THE TARNISHED STAR

Sheriff Cole Masters just wants to raise a family with the woman he loves. But upholding the law, when guns rule, is a dangerous business. When Cole arrests a rancher's son for the murder of a saloon girl, the father will do anything to free his son. And soon the lawman is on the run for murder — chased by two gunmen. The rancher wants Masters dead — but blood will run as Cole Masters attempts to reclaim his tarnished star.

JACK MARTIN

THE TARNISHED STAR

Complete and Unabridged

LINFORD
Leicester

First published in Great Britain in 2009 by
Robert Hale Limited
London

First Linford Edition
published 2011
by arrangement with
Robert Hale Limited
London

British Library CIP Data

Martin, Jack, *1965* –
    The tarnished star. - -
    (Linford western library)
    1. Western stories.
    2. Large type books.
    I. Title II. Series
    823.9′2–dc22

ISBN 978–1–44480–589–5

Published by
F. A. Thorpe (Publishing)
Anstey, Leicestershire

Set by Words & Graphics Ltd.
Anstey, Leicestershire
Printed and bound in Great Britain by
T. J. International Ltd., Padstow, Cornwall

This book is printed on acid-free paper

*For William John Martin — who
led my imagination West*

1

Sheriff Cole Masters sat there in silence, the only sound being the gentle parting of his lips as he puffed on his pipe. He took his time with the smoke, savouring the earthy taste of the burly tobacco; doubly sweet because in all likelihood it could prove to be his last. He had his feet up on the table in front of him and he reclined in his chair. He looked the image of contentment but the trained eye would see that he was, in fact, ill at ease. The sweat on his brow, perhaps, would hint that all was not well, or the way his eyes were ever alert for sudden danger.

The town of Squaw was named after an old Indian legend in which the arid land was made fertile by the tears of a squaw weeping for her lover slain in glorious battle. Once the area had been desert but the discovery and eventual re-excavation by an aging cattleman named Sam James, of a prehistoric canal system built by a long-forgotten Indian tribe had created a fertile wonder in the middle of a once barren landscape. The water originated from deep within the bowels of the Squaw Caves and seemed never ending. Some said the squaw was still there, far beneath the ground, weeping for all eternity.

It became a thriving cow town, a stopping-off point for the large herds brought from Texas and the cowboys who drove them. It was wild from the get-go with cowboys sending their herds through the streets before bedding them down and heading into town for a night of wild merrymaking in the saloons and brothels that quickly sprang up to accommodate them.

There was money in sin and as always there were plenty waiting to profit.

By the end of its first year the town claimed three saloons, two hotels, a general store, a large theatre which doubled up as a whorehouse, a corral and livery stable, as well as housing the head offices of the Squaw Cattle Company, a prosperous firm that benefited from military contracts which allowed it to stay viable even when there was an overall slump in the market. An army marched on its stomach and soldiers had to eat. Over 150,000 long-horns were driven through its stockyards during that inaugural twelve months and the growth would continue. And as the beef trade exploded then so too did the town of Squaw.

Cole stood up and felt a twinge in the small of his back. He was thirty-six years old but when he crossed his office it was with the weariness of a man much older. He went to the doorway and tapped the remains of his pipe onto the boardwalk and then stepped outside, squinting into a searing sun.

He went directly to the Majestic saloon: its doors were open no matter what the time of day or night, and went to the counter and ordered himself a whiskey. It was far too early in the day for strong liquor but he figured no one would be able to blame him.

Not with all the trouble he had facing him.

'Lovely day, Sheriff.'

Cole looked at the barkeep and offered a wry smile. 'Seems much too pleasant to die,' he said, sardonically, and downed the fiery drink in one. He held out the glass and the barkeep immediately refilled it. He reached in his pocket and pulled out a couple of coins.

'On the house,' the barkeep said.

Cole ignored him and tossed the coins onto the counter. He took the bottle from the man's hands and went over to sit in a corner seat with a good view of the batwings. There was a card game going on at the table in front of him and several men stood along the counter, drinking and laughing, but no one bothered the sheriff. He had a look like thunder upon his face and presumably everyone thought it prudent to keep a safe distance.

That was until Em Tanner came in through the batwings and spied him. The old man shook his head and came directly over, pulling up a chair and sitting opposite him without waiting for an invite. Not that he'd ever needed one in any case.

'Cole,' he said, and caught the sheriff's gaze. 'You're playing a foolish game.'

'Wasn't aware this was a game,' Cole said and poured himself another whiskey. He offered the bottle to the old man.

'You think that's wise?' The old man took the bottle from him but didn't drink from it. He held it there, staring at it. It seemed to hold some deep fascination for him as if the answer to all the world's ills lay within the amber liquid. He contemplated it as if the volatile spirit would explode at any moment.

'Don't really matter,' Cole said and downed his drink. He reached for the bottle but the old man pulled it away, clutching it tightly to his chest.

'You don't need this.' The old man said and turned the bottle upside down, pouring the contents over the floor where it immediately soaked between the boards. 'This is the last thing you need.'

Cole looked at the now empty bottle in the old man's hand. 'I'd be justified to kill you for that,' he said.

'But you won't.'

'No, I won't.' Cole agreed. 'I can always buy another. Got more need of ammunition than I have of money.'

'Leave town, Cole. Just leave town before the Bowden boys get here. No one could blame you for that.'

'Run scared you mean?'

'If that's the way you want to look at it.'

'I appreciate your concern,' Cole said and stood up. 'But the Bowdens are my problem.'

'They'll kill you. What good's one man against more than a dozen varmints?'

'Likely they will,' Cole said. Then he turned and walked from the saloon. His shoulders were hunched, as if they carried all the world's ills.

The old man followed him.

'Darn it,' the old man said, scuttling in front of him and holding his hands out to stop him in his tracks. 'You need to send for some help. You can't be expected to face off these gunmen alone.'

Cole smiled. He was fond of the old man but he didn't have time for this right now. He had enough on his mind and he shivered as he looked up and down Main Street. Soon, he knew, the cowboys from the Bowden ranch would ride into town and demand he release Sam Bowden from the jailhouse.

Only he wouldn't comply and gun-play would follow.

'Ain't nobody in town wants to be deputized,' Cole said. 'The judge is on the way and I guess the state marshal thinks I can handle the matter until he arrives.'

'That's darn poppycock.' The old man spat tobacco juice into the street. 'You'll be like a lamb to slaughter.'

'More than likely,' Cole said and gently pushed the old timer aside. He walked over to the jailhouse, ignoring the town citizens who walked by and refused to make eye contact with their sheriff. They wanted him to keep law and order in this town but now that he had come up against a sticky situation they were going to leave him to it.

It was to be expected, he supposed.

The jailhouse was a small building, just the one room with three cells at the rear so that any captives would spend their days looking out into the sheriff's office. There was a large green curtain that would be closed at night, or whenever privacy was required, so that it separated the office areas from the cells.

At the moment the only occupant was Sam Bowden and he lay on his bunk, coolly smoking as if he didn't have a care in the world. He ignored the sheriff as the lawman walked in and sat down behind his desk.

Barely a couple of minutes elapsed before the old man burst in and announced that he wanted to be deputized. The old timer stood there and cast contemptuous glances at the supine figure of Sam Bowden.

'You want to be deputized?' Cole took his pipe and thumbed tobacco into the bowl.

'Sure do. If I can't talk sense into you then I'll stand besides you.'

'Little old for the job, aren't you, Em.' It wasn't a question but a statement of fact. He put a match to his pipe and sent billows of thick smoke into the air.

'Ain't too old to shoot,' the old man said. 'I was dealing with tough *hombres* before half these cowboys were born.' For a moment the old man's eyes seemed to look into the past, to a time long gone, but then he smiled and added, proudly: 'And Indians fierce enough to freeze your blood. Ain't much that'll scare me.'

'Well,' Cole stood up and worked a kink out of his neck. 'I appreciate the offer of help and I wager you're a useful man in a fight. But as I told you already this is my problem.'

'Hell.' The old man threw his hat to the floor in exasperation. 'It's the darn town's problem. You ain't the town. You're just one man.'

'An old man and a lawman with the shakes.' Sam Bowden had come alive and was standing peering through the bars of his cell. He laughed, mocking them. 'Guess I'll be busted out of here before I know it.'

Cole turned to face Bowden. 'You're going nowhere,' he said, and his fingers brushed the handle of his Colt. 'Until the judge gets here, at least. Then you'll be going away for a few years if there's any justice.'

'I'll be out and free,' Bowden boasted. 'And you know it.'

Cole bit his lip in anger. That fact that Sam Bowden considered himself above the law rankled with the lawman. The man's complete disregard was as obvious as the nose on his face.

'You want me to shoot him, Cole?' the old man asked. 'I think I'd enjoy that.'

For the briefest of moments Sam looked troubled as he watched the exchange between the sheriff and the old man, but then he slapped the bars of his cell in disgust, went back to his bunk and stretched out, head rested in his hands. He figured all he had to do was to sit tight and wait for his pa and the boys to break him loose.

'I'd like nothing better,' Cole said and looked at Bowden with a smirk on his face. 'Wouldn't be lawful, though.'

'The law don't apply to a son of a bitch like him,' the old man snapped. 'And there'd be no witnesses besides us two. Let's drill him now and be done with it.'

'Sure,' Sam Bowden spoke without getting up from his bunk. 'We'll see how brave you are when I get out, old man. The only law in this town is Bowden law.'

'Shut up,' Cole snarled, a dangerous glint in his eyes that made Sam Bowden reconsider his situation. 'Or I'll forestall the trial and pass sentence here and now. Right between the eyes.'

2

'I don't want bloodshed,' Clem Bowden said and looked at the twelve men he had selected to go and break his fool son out of jail. Damn the boy, he was too headstrong and always bringing trouble down on himself. One day, the old man supposed, he wouldn't be able to protect him and he'd end up meeting his maker with a noose around his neck.

'What about the sheriff?' Steve McCraw asked. A big man from Texas, he had been with the Bowdens a long time and had worked his way from cowboy to ranch foreman.

'Take him down without killing him,' old man Bowden snapped, firmly.

'Could be tricky,' Steve said, running a hand through the stubble on his chin. He had the beginnings of a beard there. 'Cole Masters may insist on a fight.'

'He's one man,' Clem said. 'No killing.' He mounted his horse and tipped his hat down over his brow to keep the sun off. 'We'll get Sam out without blood,' he added.

They set off — the old man leading, with Steve riding by his side while the rest of the men took up their places behind them. They rode with all the discipline of a military procession.

Clem Bowden was fifty-five years old and a widower; his wife had been too delicate for the life out West and had never really adjusted to the hardships of running a ranch. She had been sickly almost constantly. Clem felt, with hindsight, that it had taken her twenty years to die from the various ailments that had dogged her throughout her life. Maybe she'd started dying as soon as they had arrived out West, first settling outside Abilene and then moving on to Ellsworth. There they had supplied beef to the army, making a small fortune in the process and establishing the name of Bowden as a force to be reckoned with in the cattle business.

He had met her back East — in New York. She had been the daughter of a successful lawyer and Clem had been instantly taken with her that first time he saw her walking down County Road, resplendent in her elaborately decorated bonnet and brightly coloured dress.

He had never seen a woman who had such an immediate effect upon him. She set his stomach churning and raised the tiny hairs on the back of his neck. That was the stirring of love, he supposed.

He wanted her and Clem Bowden, even then, always got what he wanted. He had introduced himself and their courtship had been surprisingly brief. They had married exactly one year to the day of that first meeting.

They had gone West with Bowden chasing his dreams of wealth and empire and for a few years things had been good. Clem had been making money rounding up mavericks and selling them on. This gave him a stake to start his own ranch. His smallholding outside Abilene had grown quickly and only a few short years later he had a ranch with over 2,000 head of prime beef.

Then came the birth of their son, Samuel, and for a blissful couple of years life was perfect.

Clem Bowden was ambitious, though, and he moved his family to Ellsworth when the cattle trade took a dive in Abilene following an outbreak of Texas fever. They stayed there a few years, again constructing a sizeable ranch, which Clem sold for a fortune to the railroad who wanted to bring their new line through his land. They then moved further west and settled in Squaw, an upcoming cow town, and Clem built a ranch of such size that it was second only to the magnificent spreads owned by the likes of the Chisums and Goodnights of the world.

The empire, though, was built on shaky ground and when Mrs Bowden died from the consumption Clem had found himself left alone with a twelve-year-old son whom they had both over-indulged. But Clem threw himself into the ranch and had little time for the boy, who reminded him of his departed wife. He'd hired a nanny for the child and spent very little time with him other than to say good morning and good night. Or to give him gifts to assuage his conscience. The boy had too much, his every whim answered, and it had spoiled him.

He could show a nasty streak if he didn't get his own way.

'This sheriff's getting too uppity,' Steve said after a long silence. 'I know what you said but I'm thinking we should take this opportunity to put him in his place before it's too late.'

Clem scowled but was thankful to his foreman for breaking his reverie. It didn't pay to ponder too much, to chase ifs and maybes. He reached into his shirt and pulled out his Bull Durham.

'Oh, we'll strike the fear of God into him,' he said, and put together a smoke.

★   ★   ★

'I'll call you if I need you,' Cole said. 'I guess you'll be a handy man to have around in a fight.'

The old man smiled, revealing tobacco-stained teeth. 'Darn tooting, I am,' he said.

'I'll come get you if I need you,' Cole repeated, eager to get him away from the line of fire. Gently he led the old man outside. He expected Bowden's men to arrive at any time and the last thing he wanted was this old man around when trouble started.

It was too late. As soon as they got outside and stood on the boardwalk, Cole's heart sank. Jessie Fuller was coming across the street, heading straight towards them.

It never rains but it pours, Cole thought, and his mood darkened further.

'I'll keep watch out here,' the old man said, noticing the woman, Cole's sweetheart, crossing the street. She seemed oblivious to the fact that the hem of her dress was dragging along the dusty ground.

'You do that,' Cole said. It didn't look as though he had any choice in the matter in any case. Not only was the old man hanging around but now he had his fiancée to contend with. Facing the Bowden crew would be difficult enough without the extra worry these two provided.

'Hello Cole,' Jessie said. She stepped up onto the boardwalk. 'I'd like to speak with you.'

Cole looked at her, frowned. He wanted to tell her to leave, to go home and lock herself in until this was all over but instead he smiled wryly and said: 'Of course. Let's go inside.'

Jessie and the old man exchanged looks by way of greeting and then she followed Cole into the sheriff's office. The old man sat himself down on the

19

boardwalk, bit off some tobacco from his plug, and waited for any sign of Clem Bowden and his cowboys.

'Well, what have we here?' Sam Bowden jumped off his bunk and stood by the bars of the cell as soon as he saw Cole and Jessie enter. 'Is this pretty thing another deputy? Old men and young women. I admire your style, Masters.'

'I've heard enough from you,' Cole said and tossed the contents of a vase of water at the jailed man. The water hit the prisoner square in the face and he cursed as he sprang backwards. He wiped his face on his sleeve and glared long and hard at the sheriff

Jessie looked troubled and Cole, recognizing this, drew the curtain to partition the office from the cells. He went to her and held her tightly, feeling the warmth of her body against his, the softness of her womanhood evident even beneath the layers of clothing she wore.

'Let him go, Cole,' she said.

Cole broke the embrace. He looked at her for a moment and then shook his head. 'You know I can't do that. He's got to face the judge.'

'Is it worth dying for?'

'He killed someone, you know that. I'm the sheriff of this town and it's my duty.'

'Duty!' She almost spat the word as if it left an unpleasant taste in her mouth. 'While the rest of the town cower away and let you face the Bowdens alone? That's a misplaced duty. That's suicide.'

'It's beside the point.' He went to his desk and picked up his still smouldering pipe and sucked the tip of the stem between his teeth.

'Release him into his father's custody,' Jessie half-pleaded. 'He'll still face the judge.'

'No,' Cole said, firmly. 'He stays here and sees no one. I've no doubt his father'll bring in some hotshot lawyer from back East and get him acquitted in any case.'

'There you are then.' She went to the window and peered outside but the street was quiet, too quiet. It seemed the entire township was expecting the arrival of old man Bowden and his cowboys and was hiding away. Cowards. The lot of them; stinking cowards. 'It's just not worth it. This town's just not worth it.'

'No,' Cole said. 'You're wrong. It's worth it if this town's ever to be a safe place to live, to raise a family. And I'm going to make sure of that. Sam Bowden's gonna answer to the law for his crimes. That's all there is to it.'

'You're a stubborn fool, Cole Masters.' It was infuriating the way he stuck to his ideals no matter what but, she supposed, that was what made him the man he was. The man she loved. It was no use arguing further, her pleas would fall on deaf ears. She knew Cole Masters well enough to recognize that.

'Maybe.' Cole crossed the room and took a glance through the door. Em was still there, sitting on the boardwalk, keeping sentry, but the street was quiet. Perhaps Bowden would not come, would let his son take his medicine for a change. But deep down Cole knew that was about as likely as snow in July.

'You've got to go now,' Cole said firmly. He smiled at her.

She nodded, resigned.

Cole took her arm and led her towards the door. 'I know what I'm doing. I'll be fine. You just go home and wait for me.'

For a moment it looked as if she would protest further but then she smiled, warmly and nodded. 'Be careful.' She kissed him gently and whispered: 'I love you.'

They were about to leave when Em came through the door like a loco bull. His eyes were bulging and spittle flew from his lips as he yelled excitedly: 'Bowden's here.'

3

'We're looking to talk with you, Masters,' Clem Bowden said. He stood in the centre of Main Street, his ranch foreman at his side. He was clutching a Winchester while his man stood beside him, wearing a pair of pearl handled Colts. There were another two men, both armed with rifles, a few feet behind them. The rest of the men had scattered to strategic points along the street.

Cole cursed beneath his breath and looked first at the old man and then at Jessie. 'You two stay here.' He took his rifle, an aged Spencer, from its hook upon the wall and stepped outside.

'Then talk,' Cole said to the rancher, feeling a slight tremor in his voice and hoping it wasn't audible to Bowden and his men. He felt his finger tensing on the trigger of his rifle and took several deep breaths, willing himself to relax. He stepped down from the boardwalk and onto the street. He glanced back at the jailhouse to make sure Jessie and the old man had not followed. They hadn't, and he stared at Clem Bowden.

'I want you to release my son,' Clem said.

'I can't do that,' Cole replied. 'It's a little more serious than shooting up the town this time. Your son killed someone.'

Clem looked down at the ground and shook his head. 'I hear it was only a whore,' he said. 'And besides, you got any witnesses my boy did it?'

'No.' Cole scanned the street. Bowden had men everywhere and there were at least six rifles trained on him that he was aware of. 'No witnesses.'

'Then what makes you certain my boy did it?'

'Don't know anyone else who'd take pleasure in cutting up a defenceless woman.'

That seemed to anger Clem. 'Woman,' he roared. 'It weren't no woman. This was a whore. Just because God gave her titties don't make her no woman.'

'She was a woman, sure enough.' Cole stood his ground, feeling the evil eye of each and every weapon trained on him. He bit his lower lip to quell his nerves and prayed that the anguish he was feeling was not visible. His muscles ached and felt as heavy as lead. He wasn't sure that he'd be able to shoot if the need arose and suddenly the magnitude of the danger facing him sent his stomach into spasms.

'My son will face trial,' Clem Bowden said firmly. 'But until that day comes I'll see him released into my custody.'

'No,' Cole said, spitting the words out of a dry mouth. The whiskey he'd drunk earlier had left a sour taste in the back of his throat and he coughed, almost hearing fingers tense on triggers as he did so.

'Well, we're going to take him,' Clem said. He nodded to his ranch foreman beside him. 'You going to stop us?'

Clem took a step forward, then Cole sensed movement behind him and he turned to see both Jessie and old man Tanner standing on the boardwalk outside the jailhouse.

Two of Bowden's gunmen were standing, one on each side of Jessie and Em, and each suddenly trained his weapon on them.

'Shit,' Cole said.

Clem and his ranch foreman kept up their steady pace and were now almost level with Cole. They didn't alter their course but kept coming with measured, purposeful strides. Clem Bowden made eye contact with Cole and the beginning of a small smile appeared at the corners of his mouth.

Cole tried to keep his panic under control but it wasn't easy and he felt beads of sweat being squeezed out of his forehead.

'That's good, Sheriff,' Clem said as he and his men approached and were now only a few feet away. 'You can't stop us so don't bother trying. Let's do this nice and peaceable.'

Cole wanted to call him a son of a bitch. Wanted to draw his weapon and face Hell itself. As long as he took that smug bastard Bowden to the grave with him it wouldn't have been in vain.

He would have done it too had it not been for Jessie and Em behind him. If he fired then they would certainly get it, either by design or in the crossfire. Cole guessed the former would be the more likely.

'I'm just going to take your weapons from you,' Bowden said. 'Don't get all jumpy and start a war you can't possibly win.'

Cole narrowed his eyes and bit down even further on his lip so that he tasted blood. He glanced again at Jessie and the old man, then bowed his head while Clem's hand reached out and took the rifle from his hands. The rancher handed it to his foreman.

'Good, good,' Clem said, then, ever so slowly, he slid Cole's six-shooters from their holsters.

'Very wise,' Clem Bowden said, turning the guns over and over in his hand while he balanced his own Winchester against his hip. He tossed Cole's Colts onto the ground several feet away. 'The keys to release my son.'

He held out a hand.

'Top drawer of my desk,' Cole said. He had to resist the urge to reach out and strangle all life from the man's scrawny neck. 'And take this while you're at it.' He pulled his badge from his shirt and slapped it down into Clem's hand. He had failed in his duty and didn't deserve the badge of office. He stood there, head bowed, feeling more shame than fear.

'You retiring?' Clem asked. He tossed the badge in his hand, as if testing its weight. 'Can't say I blame you none. The people of this town sure enough don't want to back you up. Seems foolish to put your life on the line for them.'

'Just do what you will,' Cole snarled, every syllable dripping with a thick gravy of contempt, but he knew Clem was making sense. If only one or two of the town's men had stood up and joined the fight then maybe he could have handled the situation. Bowden wouldn't have been so keen to push if he'd faced several guns rather than a lone lawman.

To hell with the town.

'No one gives a damn for one more dead whore,' Clem said. He brought the butt of his rifle twisting into Cole's stomach with sudden force, driving the wind from him in a roar.

Cole doubled up and the other man, Bowden's foreman, hit him squarely in the side of his head with the butt of the Spencer and brought up a knee into his jaw with a sickening thud. It felt as though there was a tornado inside Cole's head and his legs buckled beneath him.

Jessie screamed as she saw him fall to the ground but it sounded faint and distant to Cole, like something deep within a dream. He tried to lift himself from the dirt but his limbs refused to work and a paralysing pain ran the length of his body, sending red-hot pinpricks into the deepest recesses of his soul. He coughed, spluttered, and again tried to lift himself but he had no strength and he didn't even whimper as he felt another boot being driven into his side.

Mercifully blackness overtook him quickly and everything else ceased to matter. The very air around him became treacle and he could feel himself drifting about in a thick haze.

Cole tried to speak, couldn't.

Then . . . nothing.

4

The slightest movement caused extreme pain but Cole ignored it.

Gritting his teeth, grunting, he managed to pull himself upright.

He stood there for a moment on unsteady feet, at first unsure of where he was, how he had got here. Then it came back to him — Clem Bowden's sneering face, the rifle butt hard and cruel, the vicious blows that had rained down on him and then the darkness that had overtaken him. His stomach cart-wheeled and bile gathered in the back of his throat.

He was at Jessie's, on a makeshift bed placed on the floor. She would be sleeping in the bedroom, he guessed, and he didn't feel like disturbing her. Not at the moment. He wasn't sure what time it was and he didn't much feel like company.

He recalled coming round earlier. Jess, the old man and the town doctor had hovered over him. He'd been seeing double, was probably concussed. The doc had given him some sort of sedative to ease the hammering in his head and then he had fallen into a deep sleep.

With the recollection his stomach turned again. He stumbled outside and fell to his knees, vomiting in the street. He knew from his army days that vomiting was the result of concussion and he feared fainting away again. He bit his lip and held his head in his hands.

He lay there for several long minutes, the cooling night air having an invigorating effect on him.

Music drifted over from the Majestic but that gave Cole little idea of what time it actually was since the saloon had been known to stay in full swing until dawn. He ran a hand through his tousled hair, connecting with a lump the size of an eagle's egg on the back of his head. It smarted when he touched it and then his fingers probed the left side of his face. His eye was swollen and there was dry blood caked around a tender-feeling gash.

He figured he must look a pretty picture just at the moment.

His jaw ached too and he remembered Bowden's man driving a knee like a hammer into it, knocking him senseless. He spat, tasting blood on his swollen tongue, and then went back inside.

He crept over to the fireplace so as not to wake Jessie and felt along the mantel for the pipe he kept there. He found it and then took a tobacco jar from the cabinet and filled the bowl. There were matches with the tobacco and soon he had himself a smoke going. It was painful though to hold the pipe in his mouth and he gave it up without finishing it.

He noticed his gun belt and Colts hanging on the back of the door. He grabbed it and put it on. He looked around in the semi-darkness for the rest of his belongings, but other than his hat he couldn't see anything. If they had collected his star and rifle from the street he couldn't see them. He didn't want to light a lamp and risk the flickering light disturbing Jessie in the next room, so he grabbed his hat and went back outside.

He churned the day's events over and over in his mind. He knew that he had been put in an impossible situation. With all those guns trained on him there was no chance he could have survived had there been a fight, but that wasn't the reason he had held back — he was sure of that. It had been Jessie and the old man standing there, it was concern for their lives that had restrained his hand.

If he had been alone to face Bowden and his men he would have made a play, taken as many of them out as possible before the inevitable bullet took him down. He wasn't afraid to die, not when the principle of law was involved. He represented that law and if he couldn't stand up for it, face death and destruction on its behalf, do his duty by the badge, then he wasn't truly a man.

Yet standing there, in the cold night air, he felt like a coward. And that hurt a hell of a lot more than either the throbbing in his head or the aching in his jaw. He spat into the street, tasting blood in the back of his throat and made his way across to the jailhouse. He guessed Sam Bowden would have been released by now and he wanted to see what mess they had made of the place. Not that it mattered much to him.

He had removed his badge and backed down to the Bowden mob.

He didn't deserve the title of sheriff.

He had tainted the badge.

The jailhouse door wasn't locked and he walked straight in. Apart from the absence of one prisoner it looked much the same as it had when he had left it earlier.

It seemed like a thousand years ago now, another life-time.

'What you doing here, Masters?'

Cole spun on his feet, hand ready to draw, and looked into the eyes of the man who had delivered so much of his earlier beating. The man stood in the doorway, having come in from the street, and Cole cursed himself for his carelessness at not hearing the man approach.

'You're Clem Bowden's foreman.'

'Was,' the man said smiling. 'Name's Steve McCraw.'

'Was?' Cole smiled back even though it hurt to do so. 'You fed up with the skunk or something?'

'No,' Steve said. 'And you watch what you say about Mr Bowden. I ain't his foreman no more simply because I've got your old job now. Man can't be in two places at once.'

Cole stared at him. 'You mean — '

He didn't get to finish the sentence before Steve laughed and pulled his long coat open to reveal the tin star

37

pinned to his shirt. He wore a gun belt with two gleaming Colts in holsters which were tied down to his legs.

'Town's last sheriff weren't up to the task,' Steve said. 'So the good people elected a new man there and then.'

'You?'

'Yep.'

'Bowden arrange that?'

'*Mister* Bowden,' Steve said, emphasizing the title. 'Suggested me for the post and no one said anything against it.'

'I bet they didn't,' Cole said and pointed to the open cells. 'So did you decide to release the prisoner or was that the old man's idea?'

'Samuel Bowden will face trial,' Steve said, relishing the authority the office of sheriff brought with it and ignoring the other man's sarcasm. 'I decided to release him into his father's custody after they both swore he would remain at the Bowden ranch until the judge gets here. They are both law-abiding and honourable men so I see no problem in that.'

'Sam Bowden cuts up women,' Cole said. 'And his father just uses his wealth and position to bully people.'

'Watch your mouth, Masters,' Steve said, a glint of anger in his eye, his lips pulled back into a snarl to reveal chipped teeth. 'You ain't sheriff in this town no more and if you ain't gone by dawn I'm going to come looking for you. Now get out of here and consider it fair warning.'

Cole shook his head and poised himself to fight. This time there was no Jessie or the old man to get in the way and a much more even match. He'd be dammed if he would let this go.

Cole sneered at the other man. This was the man who had very nearly broken his jaw and beaten him senseless with the butt of a rifle. And to add insult to injury the man was now standing in his office wearing his badge. It made a complete joke of the law. It was as if the man was laughing at everything Cole held in regard, and that made his blood boil.

'Sam Bowden's a son of a bitch woman-killer who deserves to swing,' Cole said, baiting the new sheriff. 'And his father's worse.'

'Why you . . . ' Steve said and went for his gun. Only Cole was quicker.

Gunfire roared and the slug tore into Steve's chest, sending a spray of crimson into the air and lifting him off his feet and depositing him, already dead into the street. In that split second before the bullet had torn into him, McCraw's face seemed to register that he had been beat. A look of incredulous surprise welcomed the bullet that took him into eternity.

Cole went to him, bent down and took the tin star from his shirt. The bullet had glanced it as it had entered the man's chest and it was bloodstained and buckled. But he took it none the less and placed it into his pocket.

'You've been deemed not suitable for the job,' he said and quickly vanished out through the back of the building when he heard the street start to fill with people drawn by the sound of that single gunshot.

Cole had no clear idea what he was going to do next; everything had happened so quickly and he was still dazed by the afternoon's events. It all seemed unreal to him and he decided to retire to a safe distance while he figured his next move.

5

Cole hugged the side of the building and watched Jessie's place. It had been some time since the shooting and so far nobody had connected him with the deed and come looking for him, but he knew it was only a matter of time.

Jessie was awake.

Moments ago he had seen her come to her door and peer outside but she had quickly gone back inside and now lamplight flickered behind the heavy curtains. No doubt she would have made the connection with his disappearance and the commotion across the street but thankfully she had the good sense not to investigate, preferring to sit tight until she learned exactly what had happened. That gave him time before Bowden's men would come seeking revenge for the shooting of one of their own.

He felt the butt of one of the Colts for reassurance, came out of concealment and slowly walked towards the small house he and Jessie planned to share after they married. His eyes constantly scanned the street but nobody seemed to notice him and he reached the house without incident.

He quickly went inside.

'Cole.' Jessie stood up and came to him, holding him to her.

'I'm OK,' he said and led her away from the window in case someone saw their shadows. 'I'm going to have to vanish for awhile,' he said. 'Figure out what my next move will be.'

'It was you?' Jessie's eyes were wide in terror. 'The gunfire?'

Cole nodded.

'Who?'

'The new sheriff, Bowden's foreman.'

'They made him sheriff?'

'Well, he was wearing the badge.' Cole was about to remove it from his pocket but then he remembered the bloodstains and thought better of it.

'Seems to have been Bowden's doing.'

'Is he dead?'

'Yep.' Cole looked away from her eyes and breathed deeply. 'It was either me or him.'

For a moment there was silence apart from the faint sounds of raised voices drifting over from the street. 'So what are you going to do?' Jessie asked presently.

'I'm going to hide out somewhere,' he said. 'Meet the stage and tell the judge what's happened here. And then I'm coming back for you.'

Her eyes started to fill with tears and she buried her face in his chest. 'They'll kill you.' She had their wedding to look forward to but now a black cloud of hopelessness began to descend, strangling any dreams of a rosy future beneath its opaque and desolate shroud. All her plans and dreams had been turned upside down by these latest events.

'They'll kill you,' Jessie said, meaning Bowden's men.

'If I give them the chance, yes,' Cole

said. 'But they won't get that chance and I swear Sam Bowden will face trial for what he's done.'

'They'll come here looking for you.'

'Yes.' Cole nodded. He could see the worry clear in her face and he kissed her gently on the forehead. 'But they won't find me. They won't do anything to you, not with the judge on the way. The death of a whore Bowden can cover up but you're a schoolteacher. The old man won't let his men touch you.'

It all made perfect sense but Jessie felt as if her entire life had suddenly moved way beyond her control. 'I'm scared,' she said.

'Good,' Cole said. 'Fear will keep you careful.' Again he looked around the room and then asked: 'What happened to my rifle?'

'Bowden kept it.'

'No matter,' Cole said. He had his Colts. 'Don't worry if you don't hear from me for a while. The stage'll be through in four days and I'll be on it.'

'Be careful,' she said. They embraced and kissed, at first gently but then harder, passion and fear a heady cocktail, until Cole pulled away and went to the door.

'I'll be back for you,' he repeated. Then he vanished into the night.

★ ★ ★

As soon as Charley Perry had discovered that the new sheriff, Steve McCraw, was dead he had mounted up and set out for the Bowden ranch. He had worked out that Masters must have been responsible for the shooting and he knew that it was only a matter of time before everyone else figured it out too. Events like this could spark off a war and he felt he could turn that to his advantage.

Clem and Sam Bowden had returned to their ranch after the excitement with Masters this afternoon but many of their men had stayed behind in town. And given their drunken state they were apt to form a lynch mob and go after Masters just as soon as they made the patently obvious connection between him and the shooting. Which was not something Clem Bowden would want, given that his son was facing trial for the mutilation and murder of a saloon girl. It was something that the old rancher would very much want to prevent.

Charley didn't work for Bowden himself but he was sure that if he took the news to the old man he would be suitably rewarded.

It was a clear night and he was able to keep his horse in a gallop for most of the journey. Only for the last mile or so did he slow to a steady trot. His horse, although a magnificent creature, was tiring and Charley knew the importance of a good horse in these parts. It didn't make any sense to exhaust the horse when he still had the ride back to town ahead of him.

Financial gain or not, he was not going to lose his horse.

There was a guard on sentry duty at the ranch and as soon as Charley was close enough to read the Bowden name in big brass lettering on the gates, he saw the man step out of the shadows and point a shotgun directly at his chest.

'I need to speak to Clem Bowden,' Charley said, his voice a little shaky. 'I'm unarmed. I don't carry a gun.' He moved to open his coat but the man raised the deadly looking weapon further. Charley smiled and sat there, arms spread wide. The horse shifted uncomfortably and he had to whisper soothingly to calm the beast.

'Do you know what time it is?' the man with the shotgun asked.

'Somewhere around midnight,' Charley said. 'But this is important. It's about the new sheriff.'

'Steve?'

'Yeah.' Charley nodded. 'He's dead.'

The man with the shotgun staggered slightly. 'How?'

'Don't rightly know.' Charley began

to feel a little easier now and he allowed his arms to drop so he could pat the horse upon the head. 'I figured it must have been Masters.'

'The old sheriff?'

'The one and the same,' Charley said. 'Thought your boss might want to know straight away.'

The man lowered his rifle. 'Steve dead, you say.' The news seemed to have both shocked and saddened him and Charley wondered how close they had been. 'Hitch your horse and follow me.'

6

Once again Charley shook hands with Clem Bowden and smiled. The thought of the fifty crisp dollars in his shirt excited him and he was eager to get off this property and back to town. The old man seemed equally keen to be rid of him.

'Remember, anything I can do,' Charley said as the gunman who had stopped him earlier led him back to his horse.

Clem Bowden watched them go and then shook his head.

He looked at the night sky and a single star in particular as he thought of his late wife and the son they had produced between them. He had lost a good man in Steve McCraw. If his own son had been more like his ranch foreman then maybe none of this would have happened.

If it was Masters who had killed

Steve, which seemed the most likely explanation, there was no telling where this could all go.

'Damn you,' he said, cursing his wife who had died and left him with this son he had never known how to handle.

Sam came out of the house. Only a moment ago he had been in his nightshirt but now he was fully dressed. He had his guns slung over his shoulder and he stood there beside his father while he strapped the holster on.

'Where are you thinking of going?' the old man asked. He hugged his coat around him against the cold. 'I asked you a question,' he said to prompt Sam, who was simply staring at him, open-mouthed.

'Into Squaw,' Sam said as if it should have been obvious. 'I'm going to find Masters and make him pay for Steve.'

'Inside,' Clem said, noticing that several of his men had emerged from the bunkhouse now that the news had got about. They too would be eager to get after Masters and exact revenge for their departed foreman.

'But . . . ' Sam stood there, mouth agape. He looked deep into his father's eyes and knew there was no use arguing. When the old man made his mind up there was no altering it.

'Inside.' This time Clem spoke more firmly. The old man pushed his son back inside the house and closed the door. He stood on the step and then turned to face the men outside the bunkhouse. 'I want two of you men to saddle up the horses and be ready to ride into Squaw with me. The rest of you go back to sleep.'

'Is it true about Steve?' Dan Oakley asked.

'It's true,' Clem said, matter of factly, and turned on his heel and went back into the house.

★ ★ ★

Jessie hadn't slept all night and she had been relieved when the dawn triumphed over the darkness that seemed to cling on as if not wanting to relinquish the night to the day. Several times during the night she had heard sounds outside and had been convinced they had come looking for Cole, but no one had come and now she started to feel a little easier.

She wondered if the fact that no one had come yet meant that Cole had been captured in the night, but she doubted that. Somehow she knew that wasn't the case. It was as if there was some bond between them and she would know instantly if anything happened to him.

She dressed and washed in cold water out of a bowl and then sat there for some time, putting off leaving the house for as long as possible. With each second she expected someone to come calling but no one did. At last she could wait no longer and she left for the schoolhouse. She had to get on with life as normal, she told herself. If she and Cole were to survive this situation she had to stick to the daily routine, the usual grind.

There were several of Bowden's men

standing outside the jailhouse and again she wondered if they had Cole inside but again that inner knowledge told her that it wasn't so. It made no sense, though. There had to be a reason why they had not made a move to find Cole.

Something was keeping them under control.

She gasped when she saw what that something was.

'Lovely morning.' Clem Bowden came out of the jail-house and walked towards her.

Jessie nodded and willed herself to stay calm. Was Cole inside the jailhouse? Is that what old man Bowden was doing here?

'We're looking for that man of yours,' Clem Bowden said. 'Any idea where we might find him?'

Jessie knew this moment had been coming and she had rehearsed it over and over in her head during the night, but now that it came to it she felt herself falter. She looked away from the old man and took a deep breath. 'I don't know where he is,' she said. 'He left during the night.' She was aware of how false her words sounded and she was fully expecting Clem to bluntly call her a liar.

'He didn't tell you where he was going?' Clem asked.

'I was asleep,' she said, failing to make eye contact with the old man. 'He left a note. Said he was leaving town after what had happened.'

'Can I see the note?'

'No,' Jessie said and then with all the force she could muster she looked the old man directly in the eyes and said defiantly: 'It's private.'

Clem smiled but it was without humour and made the crowsfeet round his eyes deepen, giving him an almost demonic look. 'I don't believe you.'

'I can't help that.' Jessie looked away with what she hoped appeared more like indignation than fear. 'Now, if you'll excuse me.' She pushed past him. She quickened her pace towards the schoolhouse.

'Do you know Masters killed the sheriff?' Clem Bowden shouted to her back.

Jessie ignored him.

'That makes him an outlaw,' Clem yelled more loudly but again Jessie made no reply. 'An outlaw who'll be hunted and gunned down like an animal.'

Jessie continued walking straight ahead, keeping her eyes trained directly in front of her. She mumbled a silent prayer beneath her breath, praying for the inner strength she needed to get her through this.

Clem spat in the street, then turned and walked to the jailhouse, a plan fully formed in his mind.

He knew what he must do and he had perfected his plan through the night. The loss of Steve was regrettable but in gunning him down Cole Masters had put himself outside the law. He had gunned down a lawman and Clem knew that that action had changed things considerably. He had been depending on his lawyers to get Sam off with the murder of the whore, something that wouldn't have been too difficult, but all that had changed. Now it could be made to look as if Cole Masters had framed Sam for the whore killing, had actually done it himself, and then gunned down his replacement sheriff when his duplicity had been discovered. That was the hand Clem Bowden would play. All his life he had gambled but only when the odds favoured him, and now he felt that fate had just dealt him a winning hand.

He stepped up onto the boardwalk and looked at his men.

'Two of you,' he ordered. 'Ride out to the ranch and bring Sam to me. The rest stay close by. Relax but stay out of the saloon. I need you all clear headed.'

His men nodded and immediately set about carrying out his commands.

Clem stepped into the jailhouse and, feeling the need to be alone with his thoughts, closed the door.

7

Sam Bowden had spent the morning nervously pacing back and forth in the large ranch house. He'd drunk what seemed like gallons of coffee and as a result his nerves were set on edge. He felt as restless as a rattler caught on a hot rock.

Every now and then he had gone outside and looked around at the men carrying out their respective chores but he had talked to no one and had soon gone back inside. It puzzled him to think what his father was doing in Squaw and he couldn't rightly understand why the old man had forbidden him to leave the ranch.

Sure, he had the trial coming up, but that was all a formality. There were no witnesses, no one would dare come forward and even say they had seen him with the girl. It made no sense him following the agreement to be confined to the ranch until the law cleared him. Not now that Masters had gone loco and gunned down Steve McCraw.

His father had been insistent though and Sam knew there was little point in arguing with his father. If the old man said night was day then the only course was to agree with him.

When he saw the two men, Josh Redford and Ted Dryer, ride in he ran from the house with such speed that he almost tripped himself on the stoop. There was no sign of his father, only the two riders, and they were not the same two who had ridden out with the elder Bowden during the early hours.

'Howdy,' he shouted. 'Where's my pa?'

'Still in town.' The speaker was Josh Redford, a tall sinewy man who had proved himself an able worker in his five years at the ranch. 'Sent us out to get you.'

'Well that's more like it,' Sam said and ran a hand through his unruly hair.

'I'll get my horse and you two can tell me just what the hell's going on in Squaw.'

The men on horseback exchanged a glance that Sam didn't understand but he had not the time or the inclination to ponder on it. This was more like it; he'd go loco sitting out here twiddling his thumbs, not knowing what was going on in town. It was far better to be where the action was.

* * *

Jessie was finding it hard to concentrate and she knew that she was losing the children's attention. Hardly surprising, given that the text in the book she was reading was making no sense to her, words came from her mouth in a jumble and she wasn't taking in anything of what she read.

Several of the children were growing restless and were whispering amongst themselves, growing bolder when their misdemeanours went unnoticed by their teacher. Soon they were openly chattering while Jessie's voice became a monotone, ignored and unheard, drifting on and on around the small classroom.

'Children,' Jessie said, firmly and put the book face down on her desk. She took up a piece of chalk and turned to the blackboard.

The children fell silent for only the briefest moment before they started whispering to each other again. Jessie had to shout to bring them under control and the schoolteacher glared at the children. 'One more disruption,' she said, 'and someone will be punished.'

'There's a man at the window,' yelled Tommy Cooper excitedly. He was a small boy with wire-rimmed spectacles and a thick tuft of ginger hair that seemed to burst upwards out of his head like the feather of some medieval knight. 'He was looking at us.'

Jessie frowned. 'Get on with your lessons,' she said and went to the door. Her hand paused briefly on the handle and she steeled herself to deal with whatever Bowden had in mind for her now.

It wasn't Bowden or any of his men outside, but Em Tanner.

The old timer stood by the door, looking sheepish.

'Wanted to see who you had in there,' he said.

'The children, of course,' Jessie answered; relieved to see it was the old man and not one of Bowden's thugs. 'This is a school, after all.'

'It is that.' The old man scratched his head and spat tobacco juice onto the ground. 'You know where Cole is?' he asked.

'No.' Jessie shook her head and looked up and down the street. 'Not really.'

'Clem Bowden's in town.'

Jessie nodded. 'I know.' Even now she could see several of his men milling about outside the jailhouse. They didn't appear to be taking any notice of the old man and the schoolteacher and simply slouched against the wall, seemingly in their own little world.

'He's up to something,' Em said. 'He's holed himself up in the jailhouse and I just saw two of the big shots from the cattle company go in there. Don't like the smell of this one little bit.'

'What do you think it all means?' Jessie asked, leaning closer to the old man. She cast her eyes across the street but Bowden's men were still in their own world.

'Don't rightly know,' Em said. 'I'm not kin to the mind of a rattlesnake. But I wager it ain't going to be good news.'

Jessie didn't know what the purpose of this conversation was but she trusted the old man. He and Cole had been close friends for many years and he had stood beside him, been willing to fight by his side against the Bowden crew, which counted for a lot.

Especially as he was the only one in town who had offered a single iota of support to the sheriff.

'I've got to go back inside,' Jessie

said, hearing the children start up again. The more bold of her students had their noses pressed up against the window, trying to see what was going on. 'Come over to my place after school. We'll talk then.'

That seemed to please the old man. He nodded. 'Reckon I'll hang around outside here for now,' he said. 'Make sure none of Bowden's lot come over and bother you.'

Jessie smiled. 'Thank you.' She went back inside to calm the children who having taken advantage of her absence were now making more noise than a buffalo stampede.

* * *

Sam Bowden was seething.

He had arrived in town over an hour ago and had gone straight into the jailhouse to see his father. But the old man had been busy with two men from the cattle company and had promptly ordered him to wait outside; he would be summoned when he was ready for him.

Sam hated the way the old man would often belittle him like that in front of others, treating him as though he was still a buck-toothed kid.

'Treats me like I was five years old sometimes,' Sam complained, but none of the men, being more than a little accustomed to his rants, paid him any notice. He jumped off the boardwalk and kicked up dust.

One of these days he was going to show his father what kind of a man he really was.

A further hour passed before the two businessmen left the jailhouse and Sam was summoned in to see his father. He watched the two men cross the street, annoyed that they had ignored him as they left, and then went inside and slammed the door behind him.

'Father, I . . . ' Sam began, but his words trailed off to nothing as his father tossed a tin star at him. He caught it and turned it over and over in his hand as if it were hot to the touch.

'Put it on,' the old man said.

Sam looked first at the badge and then at his father. 'What?'

'You think you're a man, son?'

Sam looked at his father. 'I'm nigh on thirty, Pa.'

'I don't mean in years, son.' Clem Bowden reclined in his chair and smiled. 'I mean in here.' He tapped a hand against his chest. 'Where it counts.'

Sam stared at the badge, unsure of what was going on. 'I'm a man,' he said.

'I don't think you are. I think you're somewhere between grass and hay.' Clem said and stood up. Hands behind his head, he arched his back to work out a few kinks. 'But now is the time to become a man, so put the badge on. Or are you deaf as well as stupid?'

Sam pinned the star to his chest. 'What's this mean?'

'It means you're now sheriff,' Clem said.

'Sheriff!' Sam grinned. He didn't know what kind of joke the old man was trying to pull. 'You're sassing me.'

'No sass,' Clem said, his voice firmer. 'You've been voted and seconded by two highly respected members of the cattle company. This is an emergency situation and it is within the town's powers to elect a lawman without the usual rigmarole.'

'But — '

'There's no better choice,' Clem said, ignoring his son's protests. 'Cole Masters framed you for cutting up that whore and when things didn't go his own way he shot the man who replaced him as sheriff. You're going to bring him in, dead.' There was a long pause before Clem added: 'Not alive.'

Sam could see what his father was getting at and he had to agree it sounded a solid plan. With Masters dead they could paint events any which way they wanted. With enough witnesses the judge would think Masters had been a rogue sheriff. But how the hell he was supposed to take Cole Masters down was beyond him. Every time they had crossed swords in the past it had been he who had ended up behind bars, cooling it off in the jailhouse.

Cole Masters was many things but he was no pushover.

'You'll raise a posse and go after Masters,' Clem said. 'I've sent for two men to go with you and ensure Masters dies.'

'Men? What men?'

'Let's just say they help me out from time to time,' Clem said. 'I've used them before when I've found myself in a tricky situation. They'll be here by dawn and you'll leave directly.'

Sam nodded. He knew of the men his father referred to. He'd never actually met them but he was well aware of how his father dealt with his enemies. In the past he had seen men ride into the ranch and spend hours in the office with his father before vanishing to carry out whatever orders they had received. Nothing would ever be mentioned of their visits and this was the first time he had ever heard his father actually talk of them.

'I'll get Masters,' Sam said, bravado evident in his voice.

The plan was simple but beautiful in its brilliance. When the judge arrived for Sam's trial he would find that the accused was now the sheriff. And not only was he the sheriff, but the hero who had gunned down the mad dog Masters, a man who had shot Steve McCraw, the man who had replaced him as sheriff, in cold blood and who was also the real perpetrator of the whore killing.

Cole Masters had slaughtered the whore and had tried to set him (Sam) up for the fall.

'You'll be there, at least,' Clem said.

Sam ignored the implication in his father's words and he looked at the badge on his chest. He paced the office and stared at the cells where only a day ago he had been imprisoned awaiting the arrival of the judge.

Funny how things worked out.

'Listen to me,' Clem said shortly, his

voice taking on a harder edge. 'You make sure you pay mind to these men. Do what they tell you.'

'I'll be leading the posse?' Sam said, his inflection making it a question.

Clem ignored him and said: 'They won't take orders from you but they'll do what I tell them. They'll kill Masters and you can take the credit.'

'I'm the sheriff, though,' Sam reminded his father. 'Surely I'll be leading any posse that goes after Masters.'

'Don't be a fool,' Clem said. 'For once use the brains you were born with. You're sheriff in name only because it suits our purpose. But when this is all over, when the judge has gone, satisfied that justice has been done, we'll have a long overdue talk.'

'Yes, sir,' Sam said. At that moment he resented his father more than ever but he was smart enough to know that he had to go along with the plan. And he had to give the old man credit; it was a good plan.

A damn good plan.

8

Cole was careful not to skyline himself as he steered his horse up into the mountains. He felt sure that by now Bowden would have men out looking for him and he was determined to find somewhere safe to hide while he perfected every last detail of his plan of attack.

He needed to stay hidden for a few days before the stage carrying the judge arrived. And he was hoping the Bowdens would think he had skipped town with his tail between his legs after their showdown. They were in for a shock and Cole had justified to himself the reasons for his lack of any fight yesterday afternoon. He'd had other people to consider before himself and all sense of shame at removing his badge had been replaced by a fiercely burning anger.

71

Riding back into Squaw with the stagecoach would be risky, and could possibly provoke a further gunfight, but it was the only way Cole could think of to bring things to a head and see justice done.

Cole, of course, had killed the sheriff. The fact that the man had been rotten and only wore the star to serve Bowden's purpose and ensure his son got away with a murder charge would be neither here nor there. Technically he was an outlaw, wanted for the murder of a lawman, a hanging offence. The fact that only hours before he himself had been sheriff would count for nothing. No doubt Bowden would tell it so that it looked as though he (Cole) had been bitter at losing his job to the other man and had sought revenge with the gun.

That wasn't how it had been and Cole was going to make the law see that. As far as he was concerned he was still the sheriff of Squaw and he had killed the pretender in a fair fight. He never enjoyed killing and wouldn't unless there was no other way.

Steve McCraw had gone for his gun first, it was he who had pushed the situation the way it had gone.

He thumbed tobacco into his pipe as he rode and soon had a smoke burning away nicely. It still smarted to hold the pipe between his teeth but he ignored the pain, figured it was a minor inconvenience given that the man who had almost shattered his jaw was in a whole worse state. He guessed he could put up with his aches and pains, which were far preferable to pushing up daisies in Boot Hill.

Cole knew the country well and he enjoyed the irony in the fact that the land he now rode upon and planned to hide out in was part of the sprawling Bowden ranch. He continued to push the horse higher into the mountains, knowing the further he went the less likelihood there would be of his being found. He was careful to keep out of view of anyone in the plains below, which stretched out to an impossibly distant horizon. He guessed he was being overcautious but it was clear that Clem Bowden would want him out of the way before he could contest whatever version of events he had dreamed up. And now with Cole effectively on the run, the rancher had his best opportunity to kill him without fear of legal reprisals.

Cole cursed the day he had first set eyes on the Bowdens.

Sam Bowden had been a thorn in Cole's side ever since he had arrived in Squaw and taken up the post of sheriff. That had been over three years ago and during that time the younger Bowden had come up against him for offences ranging from rowdy behaviour to wilful damage of public property. Usually a fine would be paid and nothing more said. But this time it had been different. This time there was a body involved, a whore cut up and mutilated. Sam Bowden had been the last one with her and when Cole had tracked him down his shirt was bloodstained and his face was scratched and torn where the poor girl had fought back.

It would have been a simple case, open and closed immediately, were it not for the fact that Clem Bowden was a powerful man with friends in high places, people he wouldn't hesitate to manipulate if it served his purpose.

This was cattle country and the old man owned most of the water rights for miles around and pretty much had all the big businesses in town beholden to him in one way or another. He owned a controlling interest in the Squaw Cattle Company, a prosperous firm that held a lucrative contract with the army near by at Fort Brenner, and the bank he fronted held the papers on a lot of property in both the private and business sectors. His power was such that a proposal was currently up before the town council to have Main Street renamed Bowden Avenue. It was a proposal that everyone expected to go through the town committee with no problems. Clem Bowden had, after all, supplied a great deal of the funds to build the town hall and schoolhouse and it was he, above all others, who largely drove the local economy.

Clem Bowden, it was said, could be a ruthless man. This was a trait he shared with most truly successful businessmen, but he rarely came into town and went about his affairs in a quiet efficient way.

Samuel Bowden, on the other hand, was a different critter.

The son hadn't worked for any of the family wealth, had been born into it, had been overindulged by both his father and late mother; things had come too easy for him. He was used to having life to his own liking and he treated anyone who stood in the way of his enjoyment with contempt. He didn't care whom he stepped on or hurt, just so long as he got what he wanted.

He relied on his father's importance to ward off any trouble he found himself in. And there had been troubles aplenty.

Cole had reached a flat area, a valley between two towering peaks. There was running water and shelter from the sun and so he dismounted and allowed his horse to go over and drink. He had a sack of coffee in his saddlebags, having taken provisions from Jessie's place before leaving, and he decided that it was safe to set up a fire and camp here for a few hours.

Nightfall was still some way off and it was now entering the hottest part of the day.

An expert outdoors man, having spent hard years in the War between the States and longer still as an Indian fighter, he had a fire going within minutes. There was plenty of dead wood around, branches that had snapped from the trees during the storms of winter and now died, the moisture sapped from them, making them perfect for fuel. The water he had collected from the stream was soon boiling away.

He poured the coffee into a tin cup and carefully sipped at the bitter liquid.

Cole suddenly felt hungry and he supposed it made sense to eat now before he rested. He threw a few handfuls of beans into a pot and chewed on a piece of jerky while he waited for the beans to soften.

Afterwards he felt the need for a little sleep and he judged by the sun's position that it was somewhere around early evening. He'd allow himself a couple of hours and then move on, find a more secure hideout in the caves at the top of Squaw Ridge. He knew the caves well and there was no way anyone would have been able to approach without him seeing them. From the highest peak, near the caves, he would be able to see for ever in all directions.

The Squaw Mountains extended for miles, running clean into the next territory. Many years ago tectonic pressure had created the geological folds now known as Squaw Mountains. In some areas heat from geological forces had created formations of crystal and novaculite, the latter being a rock that was only ever found here and in the mountains of northern Arkansas. It had an ethereal, greenish tinge when the sun struck it in a certain way. Deep winding caves, like arteries, ran through the mountains, many too deep to be explored.

The horse was chewing on grass and Cole tethered it to a tree before removing his bedroll and lying down, his gun in his hand. Almost instantly he went into a deep sleep.

Long ago during his army days Cole had learned to sleep whenever and wherever he got the chance. Sometimes a man never knew when the next opportunity would come and it was important to catch what a man could. A rested mind stayed alert and in certain situations a wandering concentration, dimmed from fatigue, could prove fatal.

★ ★ ★

Em put the last of the potatoes into his mouth and used a large piece of bread to mop at the gravy. By the time he had finished and sat back in his chair his plate looked as if it had been licked clean by a ravenous dog.

'Thank you, most kindly,' he said and rubbed his stomach. He couldn't remember the last time he had eaten so well. Or, for that matter, the last time he had eaten a woman's cooking, a real home cooked meal. He tended to fend for himself a lot and the most extravagant dish he could manage was beef stew. And that usually turned out runny and left a person hungry even after consuming gallons of the tasteless liquid. Not like this stuff that stuck to a person's ribs and filled the belly.

'You're very welcome,' Jessie said. She collected the dishes and took them over to the stone sink. She placed a large pan of water on the stove to boil and set about preparing some coffee.

'You can smoke if you so wish,' she said.

'Don't indulge in that particular vice,' Em said and bit off a chunk of chewing-tobacco from his ever-present plug.

Jessie considered that chewing tobacco, which turned a person's teeth yellow and gave their breath an unpleasant earthy scent, an equally undesirable vice but she said nothing. It was funny but Cole's pipe smoke had always annoyed her and yet she would have given anything right now to smell the pungent aroma drifting through the room. She smiled and for a moment closed her eyes as she remembered Cole's customary after-dinner smoke.

'Never thought I'd miss a man smoking,' she said, as much to herself as the old man.

'You worried about Cole?' Em asked and leaned back in his chair. He patted his stomach in contentment.

Jessie was surprised at how perceptive the old man could be and she nodded while she took the now boiling pan from the stove and made the coffee. She took a cup over to the old man and handed it to him.

'Yes,' she said, sitting herself down in the soft chair beside the stove. 'I can't think of anything else. I'm worrying myself sick.'

'Don't,' Em said. 'He's doing the right thing. If I know Cole he's got every single detail worked out. It's in his nature to be careful. Never did know a man so careful.'

'You think so?'

'Yes,' Em said. 'If he stayed in town then the Bowdens would keep on pushing him until he snapped. With the judge coming to town they'd want Cole out of the way. Cole is the one man who could still put Sam Bowden behind bars and Clem'll do anything to save his rotten son.'

'If that was the case,' Jessie said, 'then why didn't they just shoot him the other day instead of humiliating him so? They had him hopelessly outnumbered as well as outgunned.'

'Too many folk about to see it,' Em said. He had no doubt that Clem Bowden would want Cole dead before the judge arrived and would have liked nothing better than putting a fatal shot into him. 'They'll try to get him on his own. When there is no one about to contradict whatever wild story they come up with.'

'It could come to that,' Jessie said. 'When Cole returns.'

Em shook his head. 'It'll be too late then. Clem won't risk anything with a territorial judge in town. That's why he's got where he is without a blemish on his character.'

The fact that Clem Bowden had taken up residence in the jailhouse troubled Em but he kept his concerns to himself. And the same fact only added to his conviction that Cole was being prudent in hiding away.

He had a good idea where Cole would be and he knew that there was little chance of his being tracked down.

He would turn up when he was good and ready.

Jessie smiled, wryly. 'Maybe you're right,' she said. 'I do hope so.'

'I'm right sure enough,' Em said. 'This'll all work itself out and you and Cole will have the biggest wedding this town's ever seen.'

Jessie went to the window and stared out at the darkness. She wondered where Cole was and what he was doing at this particular moment. She prayed he was safe.

'I'd best be going,' Em said shortly. 'Try not to worry too much.'

'I'll try.'

'Good.' The old man smiled. 'I'll call round in the morning and walk you to the schoolhouse.'

'Thank you,' Jessie said and showed the old man out. Once he had gone she stood there for a long while, her back against the door, listening to the silence.

9

Dawn sent shadows dancing across the entrance to the Squaw Caves, giving the rock its famed fluorescent glow. The minute traces of crystal and novaculite within the rock caught the sun, causing the mountains to seem alive in places. Sometimes, in a strong light, the mountains would appear to shine a deep green. It was this phenomenon that had led the Indians to attribute supernatural qualities to the mountain range, proclaiming it a sacred place. The area is mentioned in the writings of Hernando de Soto. During the European's expedition through the country late in the sixteenth century, he and his men had come upon the mountains during a particularly clear moonlit night and thereupon called them, *el pico brillante*. This translated as 'the glowing peak'.

It was just after first light and already

the sun was warming the ground. Cole, weary after guiding the horse over some tricky terrain, was relieved when he tethered it outside the largest of the caves and sat himself down on a rock. It had been slow, ponderous going and several times Cole had had to dismount and lead the horse along some of the more perilous sections which were made doubly dangerous by the fact that they were moving at night, moonlight and the strange greenish glow of the mountains giving the only illumination.

The plan was to remain here for the next two days and then move out and get into position to meet the stage as it made the final leg of its journey to Squaw. It would be nice if he could remain hidden until that time and avoid any conflict with Bowden or his men, which was why he had come here. He was hoping the men searching for him, being cowboys rather than trackers, would miss his trail and figure he'd headed towards the desert and the town of Allensville some fifty miles distant.

It seemed a reasonable plan.

And if the worst did come to the worst and a posse found him he was sure he could hold them off for days, or for long enough to make an escape and lose them in the mountains. The only weapons he had were the pair of Colts, his rifle would have given him even more of an advantage but this was a good strategic point to fight off an army, let alone an ill-equipped posse formed by Bowden.

He was hoping that the fact he was so well concealed would frighten them off. They were mostly ill-equipped cowboys and would not be so eager to get into a fight if there was a chance of most of them becoming fatalities. None of Bowden's men had the stomach for real bloodshed. There was no way of taking him by surprise. The topography of the mountains meant he would see them approaching for miles around, giving him the option of flight and avoiding a fight altogether should he so choose. That would be preferable — all he needed to do was get to the judge before Bowden did and lay out his case. He was sure the judge would sanction the involvement of the army in preventing a possible war while they took Sam Bowden in for his crimes.

Cole set a small fire and went about making a camp. He kept the flames low and the fire virtually smouldering so that the smoke would not be visible to anyone more than a mile away. And soon the delicious smell of fresh coffee was teasing him. He poured the thick liquid into his tin cup and sat, smoking his pipe and looking out at the majestic landscape.

Sitting here now, the delicious oaty taste of the tobacco drifting around his mouth, the warm touch of the sun upon his face, a landscape before him so perfect that only the Lord could have created it, it was easy to forget a person's trouble. And Cole was grateful for that. He still ached from the beating he had taken but now, perhaps for the first time, he felt truly comfortable.

Several times he thought he'd heard movement coming from somewhere in the darkness but he put it down to nerves. It would be the gentle breeze blowing through the foliage or some critter out foraging for food.

He was alone out here.

No one ever came to Squaw Mountain.

★ ★ ★

Em Tanner had been true to his word, having promised to walk Jessie to the schoolhouse so that Bowden's men wouldn't badger her none. It had been the old man's idea and although Jessie didn't fathom the reasoning of it she indulged him all the same. It seemed the old man was going to watch over her until Cole returned.

'A more despicable bunch you never did see,' Em said and scratched the back of his head. He carried a rifle and he clutched it tightly to his chest as he watched the men mount up outside the jailhouse. Sam Bowden, wearing the tin star of office, seemed to be supervising.

'What's happening?'

Em looked at the schoolteacher and then back at the men. There were ten of them in total, all heavily armed and looking like a militia. He recognized most of them as being Bowden's ranch hands but the two tall men on the powerful-looking horses were strangers to him. They sat on their mounts, looking on impassively while Sam barked out orders to the other men. One of them, a tall, powerful looking man was some sort of half-breed. Comanche blood would have been Em's guess.

'They'll be forming a posse to look for Cole is my reckoning,' Em said and spat tobacco juice.

Jessie shuddered. 'Come on,' she said, prompting the old man. She didn't like the way he was staring at the small army and feared that at any moment they would notice and challenge them. 'Let's get to the school-house.'

'Don't like the look of them two

fellas in front,' the old man said. 'The one looks half-Indian.'

Jessie looked across and immediately knew what he meant. They didn't look like cowboys at all. There was something sinister about them and she felt a shiver run the length of her spine.

'Did you know Sam Bowden's wearing a badge?'

'Yes.' Jessie nodded. 'Betty Harker couldn't wait to come over and inform me. She was knocking at my door jest after dawn. I swear that woman starts with first light and doesn't stop till dusk.'

Em smiled. That sounded like Betty, sure enough. She was the biggest gossip in Squaw. She could often be seen holding council with the town's womenfolk, they would stand around outside the general store clucking like a bunch of mother hens, berating their men folk, fuming over the ladies of ill virtue in the saloons.

'That varmint wearing a star makes a mockery of the law,' Em said and would have added considerably more had his attention not been taken by the sight of Sam Bowden walking across the street towards them. The old man's heart tightened in his chest.

'You two.' Sam adjusted his coat as he approached so that the badge was visible to them. 'I've got papers on Cole Masters. If you folks are holding back on information of where he's at then you'll be breaking the law.'

'What do you know about the law?' Jessie snapped.

Despite Jessie's fear this man standing before them stoked up her ire. She had nothing but contempt for him and all of his kind. The worst kind of men: cheating liars. She knew what Sam had done to that saloon girl, had overheard Cole and Em talking, and she looked upon him as a malignant tumour eating away at all that was good about the town. He was a cancer and his destructive reach was expanding.

'I am the law,' Sam said and ran a finger over the star he wore. 'You'll do well to remember that.' He looked at Em then shook his head. 'You too, old man.'

'We don't know where Cole is,' Em said and made sure his rifle was pointed down at the ground. He didn't want to give the younger Bowden any excuse to start a fight. One movement was all the son of a bitch needed to justify gunning him down.

Sam struck out with the back of his hand, slapping the old man across the jaw with a sound like fish guts hitting a sink. 'Show some respect when you address me,' he said. 'It's Sheriff Bowden.'

Em gritted his teeth against the pain and fought back the urge to bring his rifle up and blow the bastard's head clean off. He stumbled sideways with the blow but managed to keep his balance. 'I'll never call you sheriff,' he said defiantly, and licked a speck of blood from the corner of his mouth.

Sam Bowden's eyes appeared to be trying to squeeze themselves free of their sockets, his skin went a deep crimson and he pulled back a hand, forming a fist to follow up the slap. He was just about to swing when his father emerged from the jailhouse and called him over.

'You're lucky, old man,' Sam said, glaring at Em. 'But when this is all over I'm going to cut your throat.' He smiled and then coldly turned on his feet and went over to his father who was standing with the posse.

'Are you hurt?' Jessie bent to steady the old man.

Em pushed her away. 'I'm fine,' he said. 'Don't you be fussing.' He glared across to street to where Sam seemed to be having an angry exchange with his father. 'I'll see that varmint dead.'

They watched as Sam Bowden mounted up and then the posse moved out. The two strangers took up the lead. Clem Bowden stood watching them until they turned out of Main Street and then looked across at Jessie and Em for a moment.

He shook his head and went back into the jailhouse.

'I don't like the look of this at all,' the old man said presently, as they resumed their journey towards the schoolhouse.

'I hope Cole . . . ' Jessie started, but her words drifted away to nothing as she fought back a sudden wave of emotion.

'Don't you worry none.' Em seemed to want to embrace her in order to comfort her but he was unsure what response that would bring. Instead he tapped her gently on the back as one would a spooked horse. 'Cole is one tough *hombre*.'

In truth though, and although he wouldn't show it, Em was equally worried. It was not so much Bowden's posse, Cole could slip that lot of fool cowboys any day of the week. But those other two, the strangers with the featureless faces and cold unstaring eyes. They had the look of killers about them: professional killers. If they were going to hunt for Cole then the object was a killing and not a capture.

'We're to be married in the fall,' Jessie said, the emotion of the situation becoming too much for her and Em's emotional support proving largely ineffectual.

'You sure will,' Em said. 'That's going to be a rooting tooting shindig. I'll be taking my monthly bath just to come to that.'

Jessie smiled gently. 'You *are* pushing the boat out for us. Come on,' she said, regaining an outward appearance of composure. 'Must not keep the children waiting.'

They walked the rest of the way in silence, each brooding on their own thoughts, but each aware that the reason for the other's anguish was concern for Cole Masters. The sight of those two impressive-looking men leading the posse had troubled them both.

'Well,' Jessie said, 'I'll see you after school?'

'Maybe not,' Em said and scratched at his beard. 'I think maybe I should find Cole. Just to warn him on that posse.' He pulled some sort of tick from his beard, examined it briefly and then popped it in his mouth.

'We don't know where he is,' Jessie said. 'He told me not to worry. That he'd be safe.'

'I've known Cole ever since he got here,' Em said. 'I've ridden with him, bedded down beneath the stars next to him. I know's him about as well as I know's myself. I think I can find him if I have a mind to.'

Jessie grabbed him by the arms. 'Do you really think so?'

'Ay,' Em said. He fell silent for a moment and seemed to be thinking it over. 'I'm sure I can.'

'It might help for him to know what's happening,' Jessie said and looked towards the schoolhouse. Any moment now and the children would be arriving. 'When will you leave?'

'I'll give that posse a chance to cover some ground,' Em said. He had a better than good idea of where Cole would hide out and he was sure the searchers would go off in an entirely different direction. They would go north, which was the obvious direction for someone wanting to escape, into the desert, and on to the great wilderness beyond. But Cole wasn't trying to flee, he just wanted to lie low, and the old man was sure he knew just where that would be.

'Guess I'll leave in an hour or so,' he said.

'Be careful.' Jessie said and then, unfazed by any indication that the old man had missed his monthly bath this time around, or for that matter the one before that, kissed him on the cheek. 'Tell Cole I love him,' she whispered gently and sweetly, as if it had been Cole's ear into which she had spoken.

Em, who had never had much to do with women, though he had once been married to a Sioux, stepped backwards in embarrassment.

He wiped his cheek, then, keeping his

head looking down to the ground, rushed off.

'I'll be seeing you,' he shouted over his shoulder and made a dash for the Majestic, obviously feeling the need for a drink before he set off.

10

Sam Bowden pulled his horse to a perfect stop. He watched the other riders for a moment before shouting: 'Where we all going?' He shook his head and glared at the two men leading the posse. 'You're leading us off in the wrong direction.'

'Is that your reckoning?' asked the half-breed, who answered to the name of Quill.

The posse stood still, all attention turned back to Sam.

Sam took the makings from his shirt and rolled himself a smoke. 'Hell yes,' he said. 'We were on the right tracks. Masters would have gone into the desert and yet you've turned east.'

'I have,' Quill agreed.

'That's back towards Bowden land. You think Masters will hide out on my own father's land?'

Quill said nothing and simply smiled. He shook his head and was about to move his horse forward again when he heard Sam Bowden pull his iron. His partner, Boyd, went for his own gun but the half-breed held out a hand to stop him.

'I'm talking to you,' Sam Bowden said, holding his Colt out in a perfectly straight arm, 'God damn you. Don't ignore me.'

'Difficult to ignore you with that thing in your hand,' the half-breed said. He smiled to steady his partner who looked coiled to fill his hand in a split second.

'You trying to avoid Masters?' Sam asked. 'You some kind of cowardly Indian?'

Anger registered in the half-breed's eyes and although it was Sam holding the gun, the younger Bowden suddenly felt a twinge of fear. He stood his ground though and kept the ugly eye of the Colt trained directly on Quill's chest.

'Some men would say that's fighting

talk,' the half-breed said. He dismounted. He held out his hands, palms up and walked slowly towards Sam. 'Now put the gun down and we can discuss this peaceably.'

'We're going the wrong way,' Sam said. The Colt became heavy in his hand and he was aware of it shaking. He looked to the rest of the riders but there was no obvious help there. They just sat on their horses staring at the half-breed as he came closer to Sam. Boyd's eyes, though, were firmly on the Colt and Sam knew he would be gunned down before the smoke cleared if he shot the half-breed.

'We can talk about it,' Quill said. He took the last few steps and stood beside Sam's horse, his empty hands held up. 'Holster that weapon and we'll listen to your thoughts on the matter.'

Sam seemed unsure of himself. 'We'll g-go my way,' he stammered.

'Maybe,' Quill said. 'You put your case across. I'll put mine and we'll have a vote on it.'

Sam nodded. 'That sounds fine,' he said.

'Good.' The half-breed smiled but the only emotion in his face was a cold resolve. He was certainly not a man to be taken lightly. 'Put the weapon back in the holster. I've seen them things go off by accident too many times.'

Sam lowered the gun and then slid it into its holster. He smiled. 'I just think we're going the wrong way,' he said.

'Noted,' Quill said. He reached up, grabbed Sam by the shirt front and yanked him from his horse. He let him fall to the floor and then drove a boot into his stomach, knocking all the wind from him.

Sam rolled up in agony and tried to catch his breath. He pulled the Colt from its holster but Quill kicked him again, this time in the elbow, sending pain like electric shocks through Sam's body and causing him to drop the gun.

Quill lifted him by the scruff of the neck and slapped him across the face with the back of his hand.

'Don't ever call me a coward,' he said. 'Now mount up and let's get on with this.'

Sam remained on the ground until Quill had mounted up and started the posse off. He remained there for several moments longer, breathing deeply, before mounting up himself and following behind. His side ached and his stomach felt as if he had been gut shot. Damn half-breed had probably broken a few ribs.

* * *

Cole crouched down and thumbed tobacco into the bowl of his pipe.

He brought a match to it and watched in which direction the smoke drifted. This wasn't right, he thought, as he looked around in the darkness and realized he was very much lost. He smiled at his own foolishness. He had thought he knew this cave system as well as any man alive and yet here he was with no clear idea of which way to go.

He smoked his pipe and laughed again. Here he was hiding out from Bowden's men and he'd got himself so well hidden that he couldn't even find himself.

'Damn,' he said and puffed hard on the pipe, allowing the smoke to linger in his mouth before drifting off in a direction that suggested freedom. 'If that sure don't beat it all.'

He had wandered into the caves at least an hour ago. He'd eaten breakfast and then set about gathering wood for the fire, forming a large pile so that he had enough to last him the next two days. And then, after tending to his horse, he had found himself at a loose end. He'd spent almost an hour filing the sears, the catches that released the hammers in his guns, to improve the action of the Colts and then decided that a little exploration into the caves was the thing to do.

Hiding out from the Bowdens was all very well but it was finding something to pass the time that was the problem.

He'd explored the caves many times in the past and always enjoyed the experience. It was like stepping into a different world. It always filled him with wonder and he had visited the caves as much as he could but lately opportunities had been slim. So it had seemed a good idea to take advantage of the spare time that had been forced onto his hands.

He was familiar with the caves and knew how far into the mountains they went, was aware of how careful a man had to be not to get lost in the miles and miles of underground caves and cavernous tunnels, but for some reason he just couldn't figure his way back out. It was as if the lay-out of the caves had been altered since he'd last been here which, barring some seismic activity, was not really possible. It was far more probable that his current predicament was down to the fact that he was getting old and had been careless.

He wasn't panicking, not quite yet. On the contrary the situation seemed humorous to him. He froze when he thought he'd heard some sort of movement coming from the darkness ahead but as he listened all that greeted him was silence.

'Getting jumpy in your old age,' he said.

He'd get out of here soon.

He was sure he'd figure it out sooner rather than later. He'd just been a bit absent-minded, was all, and he needed to think about it. He sat there for some time, enjoying both his pipe and the total silence.

* * *

Em steered the big roan onto the grassland and then stopped dead and peered at what he was certain was movement against the far horizon. It was too far away for him to make it out but it looked like a bunch of riders.

'Damn,' the old man cursed, and wished he had one of those tubes that made everything seem closer. He'd used one once but couldn't remember what they were called. 'Steady, steady.' He patted the roan's neck and continued to watch the horizon.

Could it be the posse? If it was then they hadn't gone in the direction he'd imagined they'd take and were heading directly for Squaw Mountain. And that was where Em figured Cole would be holed up.

Em had visited Squaw Mountain and its caves many times with Cole and knew that the younger man felt content while wandering the cave system. He'd often said it was the last new place to explore now that the frontier was shrinking under the might of the encroaching civilization.

It was the natural place for him to go if he wanted to keep out of sight for awhile.

Em reached into his shirt and pulled out a plug of chewing tobacco. He bit a chunk off and returned the remainder to his pocket. He urged the horse slowly forward, not taking his eyes off what were merely tiny black specks in the distance.

They were definitely riders, he decided after some time, but now they had vanished.

If they were the posse how did they know where to look? Had they picked up on a trail of some kind?

He couldn't see one but then it was possible that Cole had ridden further north before turning and heading for the mountains, in order to leave a false trail for an eventual pursuer to follow. If that was the case then the posse hadn't been fooled and had found evidence that he had made a sharp turn, effectively doubling back on himself, towards the mountains.

The posse would need a damn good tracker if that was the case.

Once again Em thought about the two strangers. They had looked nothing like cowboys; the way they dressed, held themselves, suggested hired guns or even bounty killers. Was that what they were? Had Clem Bowden hired them to lead the hunt for Cole? And one of them, the one who appeared to be the leader, had been a half-breed, some sort of Indian blood flowing in his veins.

Was he the tracker?

Indians were renowned for reading the slightest clue in the ground.

'Son of a bitch,' Em said and spurred his horse on a little faster.

* * *

Cole pushed forward, having to squeeze through a section of tunnel that was so narrow he feared getting jammed in at one point. He'd remain there trapped for ever, dying of starvation or thirst, imprisoned for all eternity between the two jagged cave walls. The thought had given him a new impetus and he wriggled and felt his flesh tear as he emerged from the narrow section and came out in another cavern.

He fell to his knees and for several moments remained there, panting, catching his breath and feeling his aches and pains more than ever. His head felt cloudy and he had to take several minutes before he could even think of moving off again.

There it was, that movement again, and this time there was no mistaking it. Someone or something was moving about in the darkness up ahead. He remained perfectly still, breathing lightly, listening, but whatever had made the sound had stopped.

Cole had never been this far into the caves before and the situation was starting to worry him. He didn't know how he'd done it but he had somehow gone wrong, taken a wayward turn, and ended up in a part of the caves that previously he'd never known existed.

And he wasn't alone.

There was someone or something here with him.

Of course the caves went on for ever and there were legends of vast fortunes in gold hidden far into the bowels of the earth; this hoard was supposedly protected by the ghost of the squaw who had given the area its name. Was that what he'd heard: the Indian ghost?

Getting foolish now, Cole told himself.

None of his previous explorations had led him to this place. The tunnels he'd covered to get here were all new to him.

This section was now large enough for him to stand up and he did so, groaning as he straightened his back for the first time for several hours. He looked around him in despair but then smiled when he heard birdsong coming from somewhere straight ahead.

Mystery solved — that must have been the movement he'd heard.

He moved quickly, leaving the cavern, and found himself having to climb a precarious section of rock, gripping the walls for the sheer love of life. Twice he almost lost his footing and feared he'd fall into the cavern below. But he climbed on, gritting his teeth and then pulled himself up onto a thin ledge. As he lay there gathering his breath he was welcomed by the sight of pale sunlight flowing through a hole in the ground ahead of him. There were large twisted tree-roots and the hole had formed around them but the gap was just big enough for a man to squeeze through. Just.

Cole was about to attempt squeezing through the hole when he heard the sound of sudden movement behind him. This time it was much closer and was coming closer still. He tried to turn around but there was not enough room. He looked over his shoulder and saw the largest wolf he'd ever seen. There wasn't even enough room to draw his weapon, he couldn't fit his outstretched arm between the cave walls and his body, he was stuck like a plug in a hole.

He started shouting, hoping to scare the animal off.

The wolf kept coming and Cole saw the saliva dripping from its vicious-looking fangs; its lupine eyes glinted as the sunlight struck them. It pounced up at the ledge Cole lay on and grabbed one of the man's legs. It bit down onto the hard leather of Cole's boots and its teeth pierced the heel.

Cole kicked out with his free leg, connecting with the beast's head and causing it to whine and snap at the offending leg. He kicked again and again but he had no leverage and all he managed to do was distract the beast so that it couldn't get a clean bite into his flesh. Cole struggled, kicking frantically, and then he struck lucky and sent the wolf flying backwards off the ledge and down into the darkness below.

Cole quickly made for the hole that led to freedom. He squeezed himself through, getting stuck at one point, but pushing with his feet against the walls to force himself through. If the wolf came back now, with him trapped like this, it would be able to tear his legs off and Cole wouldn't be able to defend himself. He pushed again and came out of the hole, landing on the ground with a painful thud. Ignoring his discomfort he whooped and hollered when he found himself out in the open air.

He drew a Colt and stared at the hole

for a moment but there was no sight of the wolf. The fall from the ledge might very well have killed it but Cole doubted that. More than likely it would have been stunned and had run off back to its lair.

Cole fell back on the ground and lay there for some time, the sun warming upon his face. After so long in the darkness of the caves he could almost taste the fresh air and he closed his eyes, enjoying the sensation of the faint breeze, the birdsong, the warmth of the afternoon running through his hair and drying the sweat upon his brow. He checked his leg where the wolf had struck but apart from some damage to his boot he was fine.

After almost thirty minutes Cole stood up and looked around. He knew instantly where he was. He was a good distance from where he had camped, he recognized the trail snaking around the mountain. A large cedar tree emerged from the hole; its limbs once covered in green were now dead, like charred skeletal arms, and Cole noticed that there was fresh earth around its trunk.

He hadn't noticed it on the way up but the hole must have appeared during the winter rains, the earth washing away from the dying plant. It would fill up again when the tree finally succumbed to gravity and fell forward, the roots tearing from the ground.

He estimated he was at least a half a mile further downhill of where he'd camped. Wearily he started to climb back up. He'd have to make sure his horse was safe now that he knew there were wolves around.

Once he reached the camp he considered going back into the caves to try and figure out where it was he had gone wrong but decided against it. It would be useful to know but that was for another time. Maybe one day he'd come back here with Em and explore this new section, see where it led them.

You never knew, they could maybe find some of that fabled gold.

11

Cole figured one more day as he bedded down for the night. And then he'd move out and meet the stage. A good thing too — he was running short on supplies, had just finished the last of the beans and was coming to the end of both Arbuckles and jerky.

He kept the fire burning low and spread himself out in his bedroll. Still fearful of more wolves he kept his Colts close to hand. He filled a pipe and lay there, smoking and listening to the myriad sounds the night produced.

So far so good, he thought and wondered what would be happening back at Squaw.

How would Jessie be? Had Bowden and his men badgered her at all?

He didn't think they would have, couldn't see the point of it. Had matters been left to Sam Bowden then he was sure the man would have moved in, tried to scare Jessie into telling him all she knew of his (Cole's) whereabouts but Clem was cleverer than that. The old man was not as bombastic as his son and would never let blind rage get the better of him. In many ways that made him all the more dangerous and Cole was sure the old man would not shy away from murder if it suited him. He would ensure his own hands were kept clean though, and for that reason Cole didn't think Jessie was in any danger.

He rolled over, bone-weary from his exploration of the caves, but sleep was hard to come by and he kept churning things over and over in his mind, thinking about Jessie back in Squaw and worrying about the feasibility of his own plan.

There would be a fight, that much was inevitable, but if he rode back into Squaw with the judge he was sure that major bloodshed could be avoided. Sam Bowden would go to prison for a very long time and his father would learn that times were changing, that he didn't own the law in Squaw any more.

Cole remembered that first time he had gone up against Sam Bowden. He was barely into his second week as sheriff of Squaw. He had been having dinner with Jessie; of course he had only just met the schoolteacher then and was still very much in the delicious phase of learning things about the woman who would eventually become his fiancée and, assuming he survived all this, his wife.

He had been taking coffee prior to leaving for the jail-house when gunfire sounded in the street. He had seen the concern in her eyes and he had smiled, politely bid her goodnight, and stepped out into the street ready to do his duty.

The street was deserted, the only sounds coming from the saloon, but the smell of cordite was heavy in the air. Then Cole heard another shot coming from the direction of the Majestic, the busiest and wildest of the town's saloons. Cole had taken a deep breath and walked towards the batwings.

Inside Cole got his first real look at Sam Bowden and he didn't like the man there and then. He knew that he would come up against him time and time again until one of those clashes resulted in bloodshed; either Bowden's or his own.

Sam Bowden had several of the saloon girls up on stage, dancing to a tune played by a terrified, doleful-looking man at the piano. Sam Bowden had a large pistol in his hands, a Civil War model, and was laughing and firing wildly into the air. From the look of the place a bullet had smashed a barrel upon a shelf behind the counter and several cowboys were fighting to get their glasses beneath the pouring liquid.

'Dance, dance, dance,' Sam Bowden yelled, manically. He'd set off another shot, firing into the ceiling and sending plaster down, like snow, into the room.

Cole had stood there for a moment watching, taking in the terrified look of the girls on the stage, the anger of the barkeep, who was just that little too scared to do anything about the wayward cowboy. And then he removed one of his Colts; he always wore two, tied down to the leg gunslinger style, the result of a youth misspent, and sent yet another bullet into the ceiling.

Bowden had spun on his feet, his own gun in hand, and faced the new sheriff for the first time.

'I wouldn't,' Cole said when it looked as if the man would reach for his gun. Years of living with a gun in the hand had honed Cole's reflexes until he was as fast as the best of them.

'Do you know who I am, Sheriff?'

Cole had smiled. 'Don't really care,' he said and walked towards Bowden, keeping his gaze firmly into the other man's eyes. He didn't blink as he crossed that room.

People stood aside to let him through, parting like the waves of the sea for a holy man.

'Give me your gun,' Cole had said

and stood there before Bowden, his hand outstretched.

'What?' For a moment Bowden look confused but then he snarled and it was unclear whether he was going to hand his gun over or make a play, since Cole did the deciding for him when he brought the butt of his Colt crashing into the side of the man's face with blinding force.

Sam Bowden's legs buckled, his eyes rolled back into their sockets, and he fell to the floor and lay there as harmless as a newborn baby.

Cole had dragged him through the street that night and then deposited him, bruised, muddy, and stinking like a hog, in a cell before making out an arrest report, the first of many that would carry the name of Samuel Bowden.

And now, here in the present, Cole lay there and cursed the Bowden name. That event, and there had been many more like it, had sowed the seed that had led to the current situation.

From that first explosive meeting things had been leading to the here and now.

One time Sam had been drinking and decided it would be a mighty fine thing to ride down Main Street wearing nothing but a hat and gun belt. When Cole tried to arrest him for indecent exposure he pulled a gun and started shooting wildly. No one was hurt but Cole had to spend several tense minutes hidden behind a building while Sam shot off all his bullets.

Cole had then wrestled the man from his horse and dragged him, naked, kicking and screaming to the jail-house. It was fast becoming a home from home for the loco cowboy.

It was after that incident that Cole had first met Clem Bowden.

The old man had come storming into the jailhouse the next morning, demanding his son be released, screaming about letting high spirits go and the heavy-handed attitude of the sheriff.

'Heavy-handed doesn't come into it,'

Cole had told him. 'Your boy was shooting off in all directions, his pecker jumping every which way. It's only a miracle no one was killed.' He had then taken pleasure in pointing out to the old man that there was a small matter of a fine before he could even consider releasing his son.

Bowden had paid up there and then, peeling the bills from a large wad. With each dollar he handed over the anger in his eyes seemed to intensify until his face had the colour of a hurricane about to make landfall.

Cole then smiled and reminded the old man that his son was currently buck-naked with only a blanket in the cell to cover his modesty. He simply couldn't release him until suitable clothes were found. Why, if he did that he'd have to arrest him all over again as soon as he stepped out into the street.

That had angered the old man even more and Cole, despite his better instincts, found himself enjoying the situation.

The Bowdens thought far too much of themselves and tended to look down on everyone else as if they were not of the same fine stock as they were. It was a joy to watch the old man's pompous indignation as he stood there before the lawman. The rancher was making it quite transparent that he'd like to strangle the sheriff with his bare hands.

'Sorry,' Cole said. 'Can't have your son wandering around naked. It just wouldn't be decent.'

'I'll have some clothes sent over presently,' Clem Bowden said, then he glared at Cole. 'You're new to this town,' he went on. 'It won't be healthy for you to carry on like this.'

'Is that a threat?' Cole had asked.

The old man shook his head. 'I'm just suggesting you familiarize yourself with the way this town works.'

Cole shook the thoughts from his mind and closed his eyes. Things had got far worse now and the Bowden situation was so far advanced that it would take blood to end it.

He willed himself to sleep.

Tomorrow he planned on setting out. The stage would be due and he needed to meet it, explain to the judge what was happening and then, if all went well, divert things, if needed, some twenty miles south to Fort Brannon and get the army involved.

Soon he was asleep.

12

Sam Bowden glared at the half-breed.

'I say we're going on a wild-goose chase,' he said. 'We're following a trail only you can see. I say you're loco.'

His beating yesterday had left him bruised and aching, it was painful to ride, but it had taught him nothing. He had simply had enough and was going no further. He wasn't going to threaten the men again but he was turning back. 'I'm finished with this,' he said. 'If you think we're on Masters' trail then I say you're roostered.'

'It's of no consequence to me what you say,' said the man called Quill. He didn't bother looking at Sam as he spoke and instead kept his attention directly in front of him. The large black horse he rode seemed to understand the conversation and it snorted in Sam's direction.

'He's a regular croaker,' the man called Boyd said to the half-breed and they both smiled at the joke.

Sam allowed his horse to fall back so that there was some distance between him and the two men in the lead. He looked at the seven men his father had selected to form the posse but none would make eye contact with him. He cursed beneath his breath. He wasn't about to find any support amongst his own men and he didn't fancy his chances of going up against Quill and Boyd on his own. Not after the last time. It seemed he had no option but to allow them to continue to lead this wild goose chase. Reluctantly he spurred his horse forward.

They had followed Cole's trail north from Squaw. That made good sense since any man trying to flee would head for the desert and the town of Allensville beyond. But then for no apparent reason other than the stinking half-breed's claiming that he had located tracks that no one else could see they had changed direction. And now they rode towards Bowden land, the Great Plains and the mountain range beyond.

That made as much sense as putting a rattlesnake in your underwear, as far as Sam was concerned. Why would Cole choose to hide out on Bowden land? Surely he'd want to get as far away as possible from the men he was trying to flee?

They rode on in silence. Day started to fade away and night began to take hold. Soon even Sam's private mutterings grew silent but his mood remained darker than the coming night sky.

★　★　★

The posse had stopped and set camp for the night.

Em, wanting to sneak past them and reach Cole before they did, had not. He was now getting perilously close to them and walked, leading his horse, all the while whispering soothing words into the roan's ear so as not to spook her. He breathed slowly, quietly and felt that if he reached out in the darkness he would be able to touch each and every member of the posse.

A while back it had become obvious that the posse had picked up on Cole's trail and were following it to the step. Em could see from the direction they had taken that Cole had tried to lay a false trail of sorts but he had not fooled them. The two men leading the riders knew what they were doing and could read the land as if it were a book written in a language known only to them. They saw things that other less well-trained eyes would skirt clean over.

Em still had one advantage, though. They were following a trail but he knew exactly where it would lead them. They couldn't track Cole at night and had to rest, both themselves and their horses. Whilst he, on the other hand, had no need to follow faded tracks, to peer for snapped foliage, for disturbed ground. He knew where Cole was and with care he would be able to pass the posse and get there before them.

And so he set off for Squaw Mountain along his own trail, keeping as much distance between himself and the posse as was possible. But now they were camped some fifty or sixty yards away from him, in earshot at least.

He could turn, follow the river some way down and then try to cross but the waters were up and fierce at any time of year. Attempting to cross in daylight would be bad enough but doing so at night would equate to suicide.

No, there was only one safe place to cross, one single section where the waters were low enough not to sweep both man and horse away, and that would take him closer than was comfortable to the posse.

They would have a man on watch; they wouldn't risk not posting someone, but Em was hoping the lookout would be complacent, not concentrating and maybe even dozing. After all, they would not feel themselves to be in any danger and that could make them careless. If he took his time and moved with the utmost care he was sure he could slip by the posse without being noticed.

He crouched down in the grass, pulling the roan's head down with him. He kissed the horse on the side of the head and whispered softly in its ear. He had to take his time, slowly move forward, but he needed a moment to gain his breath.

He took the plug of tobacco from his pocket and bit off a sizeable chunk.

'I've found myself in some darn worrisome situations,' he whispered to his horse. 'But this one tops them all.'

The horse seemed to roll its eyes in agreement.

Cautiously the old man moved forward, one step at a time with a pause to listen out between each. The horse came obediently behind him and Em was terrified that at any moment it would make a sound and bring the men investigating. The roan, though, seemed to be as eager not to get spotted as the man was and it moved in perfect rhythm with its owner. At one point Em heard a twig snap beneath his feet and it sounded deafening to him, like a cannon roaring off. He'd frozen immediately and his hand found his rifle in its boot but he seemed to have got away with it.

He sighed his relief.

If Em Tanner had stopped and analysed his feelings at that moment he would have realized with no small surprise that he was enjoying himself. Sure he was scared, the fear gnawed away in the pit of his stomach and left him feeling sickly, but it had been a long time since he had found himself in a situation of great danger, where he had to rely on his wits to survive. It was like one of the adventures he'd had of old and at that precise moment the years fell from him and he was young again.

Suddenly he heard a sound, a man coughing and he crouched down deeper into the grass. He pulled the horse's head down with all his might and then pushed his entire weight against her neck, forcing her to the ground. He lay across her, holding her down. It was an old outlaw trick but Em hadn't travelled the owl-hoot trail for decades and he was surprised that the horse went down so easily.

Guess you've still got it, old man.

The coughing stopped but then he heard movement ahead. One or more of the posse were up and walking about and he heard grass rustle as the man came closer towards them.

For several seconds, each seeming an agony-filled age, Em lay there, soothing the horse, holding it still. Any longer, he knew, and the horse would try to get up and out of this unnatural position. If that happened then all hopes of reaching Cole before the posse would be dashed.

As he lay, spread across his horse, he gave a silent prayer and hoped that his maker wouldn't hold it against him that they had not been on speaking terms for so long. He promised to stop cussing, drinking and to visit church every Sunday. All he wanted in exchange was to get past these men without being spotted.

Whoever it was moving about started coughing again and then cursed as he fumbled with his trousers. Em lay there, not sure how far away the man was, but he could clearly hear him urinating into the long grass. Any closer and he feared he'd get splashed by the urine bouncing from the ground.

After some time the man turned and headed back to camp and after even more time there was silence again.

Em, heart hammering in his chest, slowly got up and allowed the horse to come with him. Again it didn't make a sound and the old man patted the side of its head.

Best horse he'd ever owned.

Slowly but surely man and horse moved through the long grasses and Em had to bite back a whoop when at last they reached the river. He mounted the horse and held it there, still for a moment, listening for sounds of the posse but he guessed he'd got away with it. All he had to do now was cross the river and then he would be too far away for the posse to hear him.

With luck he would be able to put a few miles between them before dawn.

'Ready girl?' Once more he patted the horse's head then spurred it onward at a slow pace. They crossed the river cautiously; hoping the noise of the running water would conceal the sound they made as the horse waded through.

Once on the opposite side Em smiled and bit off another piece of tobacco from his plug. Then he allowed the horse to trot a little further before quickening its pace. He spurred the horse gently in the side and she increased speed. Once he deemed himself out of earshot he sent her into a gallop, feeling the wind in his hair as his heart-beat slowed to normal.

'You've still got it, old man,' he said,

speaking as much to himself as the horse, as he left the danger of the posse behind. 'Could teach them young whippersnappers a thing or two.'

After a while he slowed the horse down again and kept it trotting forward at a steady but comfortable pace. There was still a way to go and he didn't want to exhaust the roan. She had been ridden hard since he'd set out from Squaw and the horse going lame on him would be the last thing he needed.

He kept up the same pace for the rest of the night and as the onset of dawn made itself known Squaw Mountain appeared in the half-light. Through the early-morning mist the old man could see the mountains reaching towards the sky, majestically silhouetted against the fiery horizon.

The long-grassed plain stretched the seven miles or so to the mountains and Em guessed that in a couple of hours he would reach the mountains and start the hazardous climb.

He'd been there before, many times,

and he knew that you could ride a horse almost to the peak, but it took time and great care as some of the sections were dangerously tricky and would cause problems for a mountain goat, let alone a horse.

13

Enough was enough, Sam Bowden thought, as he shook the dirt from his bedroll and tied it to his horse. This was it and despite his earlier confrontations with the half-breed he was not taking another step.

'I ain't going another inch,' Sam Bowden said and spat into the campfire. The rest of Bowden's crew had mounted up and were ready to follow the two men who had led the posse from the get-go. Neither of the men had said very much, other than to issue a few commands. When they did talk, it was usually to each other and then only in hushed tones, excluding the rest of the posse.

The taller of the two men, Quill, the half-breed, drove his horse forward towards Sam and looked down at him the way a stern master might regard a wayward child.

'This is getting tiresome,' he said.

'I ain't going no further with you. I mean it this time.'

'Whatever pleases you,' Quill said. 'You can take some supplies and head back to Squaw if you've a mind to.'

'Damn,' Sam tossed his hat onto the ground. He kicked dirt and clenched his fists. 'Where the hell are we going? That's all I want to know — where the hell are we going?'

The tension between him and the two men leading the posse had intensified these last couple of days and Sam was close to breaking point. He couldn't understand why his father seemed to have so much faith in them.

'We're following the man's trail.' Quill said.

'Trail,' Sam all but screamed. 'We left the goddamn trail a ways back. Why would Masters be heading onto Bowden land? The last place he'd want to go is onto Bowden land.'

'We're following his trail,' Quill repeated, completely disregarding Sam's opinion.

He cast an eye to his companion and something seemed to pass between them, as if with a mere glance at each other they could convey volumes. It was as if they had a secret language based on gestures to the exclusion of words. Sam found it all creepy.

'Son of a bitch,' Sam mumbled, feeling he'd like to drag Quill from his horse and stamp some respect into him. Just as the half-breed had done to him. 'I'm the goddamn sheriff. I should lead this posse. You should answer to me.'

Quill simply smiled at that and drove his horse to the front of the posse. 'Please yourself,' he said over his shoulder.

Sam stood there, incredulous. He watched the posse start to move out without him. He pulled his Colt from its holster and fired it twice into the air. The riders stopped and all heads turned to face him. He holstered the weapon and wiped his mouth on the back of his hand.

'I'm the sheriff,' he repeated, firmly.

'I'm the only one with any real authority and by damn I'll lead this posse.'

Quill smiled. 'Then lead, Sheriff,' he said.

That seemed to throw Sam and for a moment he seemed unsure of himself. He mounted his own horse and looked directly into Quill's eyes. 'Then we turn back,' he said. 'This ain't no trail you've got us following. We go back and pick up on his real trail, follow that. Then we'll find Masters.'

'You go whichever way you want,' Quill said. 'Take the others with you but we go our own way.'

'You speak for the two of you?'

'He does,' Boyd said.

'My father hired you to ride with the posse,' Sam pointed out.

'No.' Quill shook his head. 'Your father hired us to find Masters. The posse's for your benefit, to make it all nice and legal for the judge. We ain't working for no law and if we were I don't think it'd be for a law like you.'

'We'd make better time on our own,' Boyd put in and nodded to his companion. He allowed his coat to fall open, showing his weapons, which he wore crossbones style across his stomach, in a red sash.

'Guess we might at that,' Quill said as if considering the situation. Escaping Bowden's constant whining would be a big bonus.

'Goddamn you,' Sam said. 'I ought to beat you real good. Teach you a lesson.'

'You try.' Quill opened his coat to reveal his own guns. Unlike his companion he wore a more traditional belt and holster. 'You'd be the one to go to hell.'

Sam didn't like the way the half-breed was talking to him but he decided against any action. He'd not done so well the previous time they had clashed and there was something about the two men that worried him.

'You two can go to hell for all I care,' he said. 'The rest of you are coming with me.'

The remainder of the posse seemed unsure of what to do for a moment, but then, deciding that Clem Bowden called the shots and that Sam was his son, which in their eyes gave him more authority than the badge he wore, they turned and rode with him.

They rode off in the direction they had come, leaving Quill and Boyd to follow their own path.

'He's got his father's temper,' Quill observed after they had watched the posse riding into the distance.

'Difference is,' Boyd said, 'he doesn't know how to control it.'

'Maybe he'll learn.'

'Nope,' Boyd scoffed. 'No chance of that happening. He'll end up dead before he ever learns anything.'

'Had a good mind to kill him myself.' Quill laughed. He brushed a wisp of thick black hair from his eyes and tucked it beneath his hatband.

'I guess killing would improve him some.'

'Dead — he'd certainly go up in my

estimation.' Quill took the makings from his saddlebags and rolled a smoke. 'Don't think his father would be very pleased with that outcome.'

'Guess not,' Boyd agreed. 'Damn shame, though.'

And then without another word they rode out, setting their horses to a casual trot as each of them scanned both the ground beneath them and the land before them. They figured they weren't too far away from catching up with Masters, and the fact that Bowden's boy and the rest of the posse were not with them didn't really bother them. As Boyd had pointed out, they would make better time on their own, and as long as they killed Masters and gave the credit to Sam Bowden they would have done the job they had been paid for.

Doing the job they had been paid for mattered to them.

It mattered above all other things.

★ ★ ★

Cole had noticed the lone rider some time ago and he crouched down, resting against a large rock and watched. The rider was still too far away for identification but he seemed to be heading directly this way. He checked both his guns and filled each chamber. He also took a handful of shells from his saddlebags and slipped them into his belt. Once again he wished he had a rifle but there was no use moaning. He had the two Colts and would make do with them. And besides, in Cole Masters' hands a Colt was as efficient as the truest of rifles.

He filled his pipe and brought a match to it, smoke billowed from the bowl and drifted lazily on the still air.

'Damn,' Cole muttered to himself.

He supposed he could jump on his horse and flee down the mountain. He had been going to leave later today in any case, in order to rendezvous with the stage. The rider was far enough away for Cole to have vanished down into the mountains before he got anywhere close, but to do that he'd have to go some way in the wrong direction from where he needed to be.

Of course there was always the chance that the rider could be just a harmless saddle-bum with no interest whatsoever in Cole Masters. But that seemed unlikely, indeed the remotest of remote possibilities.

He smoked the pipe slowly and as the rider neared Cole began to realise that there was something familiar about him. He was still too far away to be seen clearly but Cole recognized the way he sat in the saddle.

There was also no mistaking that horse, that roan.

'Damn you, Em Tanner,' Cole said, and started down the mountain to meet the old man.

14

'Damn you, you nearly caused my heart to jump out through my mouth,' Em said, clutching his chest and trying to catch his breath. 'Scaring a man like that. Damn fool thing to do.'

He was exhausted from the trek of what seemed like miles, all of it on the upward. He had been walking and leading the roan. It didn't help that the horse had been reluctant to take every single step and several times had tried to pull back. The higher they had gone the more determined the horse had become to go back down.

Cole, who had just jumped out from behind a large berry bush, startling the old man, laughed.

'Take a lot more than a scare to finish you off,' he said. 'Now, what you doing way out here, old man?'

Em sat down cross-legged on the

ground and wiped his brow with the back of a hand. He was panting and looked as much in need of a rest as a man ever did. He took several deep breaths.

'There's a posse on your tail,' he said.

'Figured there might be,' Cole answered. 'But they won't come here.'

'They're coming.' Em bent over and coughed, spittle sticking in his beard. He wiped his mouth with the back of his hand. 'I snook past them a ways back,' he went on and spat. His breathing relaxed slightly as he regained his puff. 'They'll be here by noon.'

Cole looked into the distance but there was no posse to be seen. The land looked so peaceful, so comforting. There was nothing between them and the horizon but more and more land. It looked like a wondrous vista stretching out before them in every direction. It was so still it could well been an oil painting.

'A posse,' he said, thoughtfully. 'Must be a damn good one to track me out here.'

'It's being led by two men I've never seen in Squaw before. They look like professionals, bounty killers maybe. I think one's a Mex or a Comanche. Couldn't be too sure with the glimpse I had of him.'

'Bounty killers?'

'Could be,' Em said. 'Or simply hired guns. Either way I don't think they'll be wanting to arrest you. They've got eight of Bowden's men with them including the new sheriff.'

'New sheriff?'

Em nodded. 'Sam Bowden,' he said. 'Plumb loco as it all sounds, Sam Bowden is the sheriff of Squaw.'

Cole grinned coldly.

Sam Bowden, wearing the badge. It was beyond belief and mocked the very core of the law. Sam Bowden was a nasty sadistic little coward and now he wore the tin star. He knew Clem Bowden would be behind this and he could see the reasoning in his making his son sheriff. It was simple, really. But brilliant in its simplicity.

'How many in total?'

'The two men, Sam, and seven others. Ten men in all. They're all heavily armed.' The old man shivered. 'I've not seen men so well-armed since the Indian wars. I reckon that posse is carrying more arms than Custer took to the Big Horn.'

Cole looked at him. 'Ten men, you say.' He hadn't quite been expecting this. He wasn't really sure what he had been expecting but it certainly wasn't this.

'Let's get up higher,' Cole said. 'See if we can see them approaching.'

This hadn't been in Cole's plan. He hadn't seriously considered that anyone would find him out here and had thought it only the remotest of possibilities. Of course, he'd realized that Em would be able to figure out his whereabouts if he really thought about it, but for someone to actually track him, to follow him to the mountain range: that was something he hadn't given any serious thought to.

He'd been so careful too, first laying that false trail and then covering up as many of his tracks as possible. Whoever was leading that posse, they certainly knew what they were doing. A Comanche, Em had said, and that would figure — the Comanche people could track a snowflake in a blizzard.

The old man had been right. This did stink of bounty killers.

'We'll be in a perfect spot to hold them off,' Em said.

'Sure,' Cole agreed. 'But that don't serve my purpose. I've got to meet the stage. Speak to the judge and sort this whole damn mess out. If we get into a shooting match it'll quickly turn into stalemate. It could go on all day or until one side runs out of ammunition.'

'Which will be us,' Em pointed out. ''Less you got an armoury hidden away somewhere around here.'

Cole shook his head and looked steely-eyed to the far horizon. Still all was still. 'I'm going to meet that stage.'

'And if the posse tries to stop you?'

'Then we'll have a war,' Cole said and his words were colder than any he'd ever spoken before. A fierce, stripping wind came with those words.

Bloodshed was still to be avoided if at all possible but Cole was not going to let anyone stop him in what he had to do. He'd meet the stage, get Sam Bowden locked away, and in doing so break the Bowdens' influence on the town.

With the Bowdens' hold on the town a thing of the past maybe the citizens would stand up and speak out.

Make a town folk would be proud to call home.

Law and order couldn't exist if even one solitary man was beyond its power. The law had to be absolute and no one could stand aside from its reach.

This all had to end and end soon.

Cole planned to marry Jessie and build a solid future for them both. He'd been a drifter all his life, spent far too long in the saddle, and he was ready for some stability. The thought of a comfortable home, a loyal wife waiting for him at the end of the day, was a good one; it was all he wanted out of life.

His saddle-bum phase was over and now he intended to shape the future in a way that suited him.

He'd be damned if he'd let the Bowdens or anyone else jeopardize that.

'Damn,' Cole said, not realizing he had spoken aloud.

It was slow going.

Alone, Cole could have covered the distance in half the time, but the old man's roan took some coaxing to negotiate the more severe sections of the mountain. Cole had never seen a more ornery horse.

They continued their trudge upwards, leaving the tree line and entering an area that seemed to consist entirely of rock. After some forty or so minutes of hard climbing they stood outside the caves where Cole had made camp.

'You made yourself at home,' Em remarked, pointing to Cole's bedroll, which was still on the ground next to the remains of the previous night's fire. The coffee pot was still hot and the old man went to it and lifted it, cursing when the handle burned his hand.

He tore a piece of his shirt and used that to lift it.

'A regular home from home,' Cole said, and went to his lookout point. From here he could see for miles and there was still nothing on the distant horizon. For a second he thought he saw movement in the heat haze that hung over the land but there was nothing.

He was getting jumpy and his imagination was getting the better of him.

'Ain't no one to be seen,' Cole said.

'I got a few hours' start on them,' Em replied. He tethered his horse beside Cole's. Carefully he sipped at the coffee, straight from the pot. 'They'll be here soon enough.'

'This puts a new slant on things,' Cole said. He started to fill his pipe.

Em came over and stood besides Cole. 'We could cut and run for it,' he suggested.

Cole sucked his pipe into life. 'Might turn out to be the only thing to do,' he replied. 'Though I would prefer not to have a posse on my tail when I stop the stage.'

Cole wondered about making a break for it and trying to keep ahead of his pursuers but the stage wasn't due near this area until noon tomorrow and the posse would catch up with him before then, forcing a fight.

It was starting to look even more unlikely that he'd be able to avoid a fight of some sort, but out in the open it could turn into a bloody war.

They were outnumbered: just the two of them against ten heavily armed men.

Some kind of showdown was inevitable, always had been.

Cole knew that if he were to have any chance of survival he had to shorten the odds in his favour.

'Damn you, Samuel Bowden,' he said, speaking more to the absent Bowden than the very present old man.

'So what'd you reckon on doing next?' Em asked. He put the last of his chewing tobacco into his mouth. 'If I got to meet my maker I'd like to have some baccy to take with me.'

Cole continued to watch the distant horizon for any sign of movement. The sun was high now and the heat haze blurred his vision. 'We may both be shaking hands with the maker before the day is out,' he said.

'Hell, no,' Em said. 'That ain't going to happen. I promised Jessie I'd get you home safe for the wedding. Don't want to die with a woman mad at me. I'd never rest in peace.'

Despite the situation, Cole laughed.

* * *

'You think it was Masters?' Boyd asked and swiped at a fly that was bothering him. He rolled and lit a quirly and pulled his hat down over his eyes to ward off both the fierce sun and the troublesome insect.

'No.' Quill stood up and brushed the dirt from his knees.

They had noticed the fresh tracks as soon as they'd crossed the river this morning. They were not more than a few hours old, which meant that whoever had made them had passed by the camp during the night. If the posse hadn't split the sentry would have been feeling Quill's wrath.

'This is a much smaller man,' Quill said. 'A different horse, too.'

Boyd looked around them and then cast his eyes back to the river. He watched the waters for a moment.

'Who?' he asked.

'Don't know,' Quill admitted. 'Don't really twig to this at all.'

'Someone going to help Masters?'

Quill shrugged his shoulders. 'Maybe,' he said. 'But I can't think how that's possible. Unless whoever it was has been trailing us while we've tracked Masters. Maybe we're getting old and losing our touch.'

Boyd shook his head, then climbed onto his horse.

'Guess we'll know soon enough,' he said and spurred the horse forward.

Quill took a last lingering look around before also mounting up and following his partner. He urged some speed out of the horse to catch up with the other man and steadied the beast when he drew level.

'Let's wind up this business and go home,' he said.

They rode, as was their custom, in silence, but the fresh tracks troubled Quill and he tried to think what they could possibly mean. There was no doubting that someone had come past their camp during the night and seemed to be heading, like them, towards Masters.

Question was who and why?

There was a slim chance that it was just some saddle-bum who had passed by and not noticed the resting posse, that there was no connection with Masters at all, but he didn't believe that. No matter how careless the sentry had been he would have heard a rider stumbling through. The sound of a careless rider would have woken the entire posse.

Whoever these fresh tracks belonged to, there was no doubting the fact that he was an ally of Masters. And, more than that, he had slipped past them with the utmost care. Clem Bowden hadn't mentioned Masters having any possible compadres but these tracks sure weren't made by a phantom. The situation had suddenly changed and now, with the departure of the rest of the posse, it made the numbers more or less equal.

'We're getting close,' Quill said. 'I feel we'll meet up with Masters before sundown.'

Boyd nodded and looked at the distant mountain range. 'Plenty of cover for a couple of men up there.'

Quill looked ahead in silence, his eyes becoming slits as he surveyed the distant mountain range. His nose seemed to twitch as if he was testing the very air for the scent of Masters and the unknown rider.

'That's where we'll find them,' Quill said.

He knew the Squaw Mountains well and was aware of the many possible hiding-places there were for a man to conceal himself. The caves alone, famous in the area, ran for miles and miles beneath the ground, but there were enough secluded places around the mountains to hide an entire regiment, let alone a couple of men. If a man had a mind to, he could stay hidden for ever.

'Masters knows what he's doing,' Boyd said, breaking the silence. 'Don't suppose he's as much of a greenhorn as Clem claimed.'

Quill offered a grim smile in reply.

Tracking would be difficult once they started going into the mountains and if Masters knew the area, as he guessed he must, then it would prove nigh on impossible to find him amongst the miles and miles of mountains that ran clean into the next territory.

If a man didn't want to be found there were ways to ensure he remained hidden in the mountains.

'Might be a little harder than we expected,' Boyd said. He slid a gleaming Winchester from his saddle boot. He checked that the gun was loaded, tested the action, and slid it back into the boot. The gun looked new, a virgin weapon, when in actual fact it was several years old, such was the attention Boyd gave to its maintenance.

'Let's just get the job over and done,' Quill said. 'I'm getting too old to be sleeping in the open.'

'Just pointing out the fact that we might have to negotiate a little more money from Clem Bowden,' Boyd said with a grin. 'Especially with his fool son and men running out on us.'

'Leaving us all on our lonesome,' Quill said.

'Just the two of us to face the music.'

Quill grinned. 'Just the way we like it.'

'Sure is,' Boyd agreed. The two men exchanged glances that were wholly private and would have been strangely troubling to any onlookers. Boyd rolled and lit another quirly and drew the smoke deep into his lungs, letting it escape slowly through his teeth.

'I'm getting kinda eager to meet up with this Masters fellow,' he said, presently.

'And whoever these fresh tracks belong to,' Quill reminded him.

'Killing's killing,' Boyd said. 'Don't make much difference if it's one or two.'

'Guess not.' Quill nodded and checked his own weapons. Quickly, with the skill of a man familiar with guns, he checked both pistols and his own rifle, a battered-looking Remington that fired true to sight despite its gnarled appearance.

'Then shall we dance with the Devil?' Quill said and kissed the butt of his rifle. He slid it back into its boot.

Boyd said nothing but the lopsided smile that failed to reach his eyes spoke volumes.

They both spurred their horses into a gallop and rode as expert horsemen, forcing their respective mounts to display all the speed of their pedigree. The grasslands between them and the mountain range blurred beneath the galloping hoofs.

15

Fear was tangible in the air.

The feeling of foreboding hung over the town like an oppressive cloud.

Folk went about their business as usual but everyone seemed quieter than was normal, as if each carried their own shame within their hearts. Each did what they had to do and then got off the street and back to the safety of their home as quickly as was possible. The heavy Bowden presence in town had everyone on edge.

Jessie stood outside the schoolhouse while the children took their morning break by running around the school grounds and scrambling over the climbing frames and swings that a few of the townsmen had constructed for their use.

She looked down onto Main Street and shuddered when once again she saw Clem Bowden and two of his men riding back into town and heading directly to the jailhouse.

Two days had passed since the posse had ridden out in search of Cole with Em following behind them at a discreet distance. To Jessie's knowledge Clem Bowden had mostly remained here in town. The old man seemed to have made the jailhouse his base, which, she supposed, he was entitled to do seeing as how his son was now the town's sheriff.

'Morning.'

Jessie had been lost in thought and she looked up to see Betty Harker standing by the school fence. She was carrying a basket containing groceries and she had a thick shawl draped over her shoulders despite the heat of a still young day.

'Good morning,' Jessie said, smiling, wondering what snippet of gossip Betty had to pass on. 'Wonderful day.'

'The children seem to be enjoying it,' Betty said. She looked over at them.

They were full of the vigour of youth, living each moment to the full, not a care in the world. 'Personally I don't like this weather. Too many flies about,' she observed.

'Yes,' Jessie answered, but her attention was taken by the sight of two of the men coming out of the jailhouse and crossing over the street towards the Majestic. There was, as usual, no sign of Clem Bowden emerging. He seemed to spend most of his time in town cooped up in that jailhouse.

Betty, noticing the schoolteacher's preoccupation, cast a look over her shoulder and saw the two men as they entered the saloon. 'It brings shame on this town,' she said. 'It truly does.'

'Yes.' Jessie nodded.

'Must be hard on you. Now that they've run Sheriff Masters out of town.'

'They didn't run Cole out of town,' Jessie snapped.

'No?' Betty smiled sympathetically. 'Then where is he?'

'He's . . . ' Jessie said but her words trailed away to nothing as she wondered just where Cole was, even if he were alive or dead.

'He was a brave man,' Betty said, as if echoing the schoolteacher's fears that he might be dead. 'I don't hold with what some folk are saying about him.'

'And just what are some folk saying?' Jessie asked. The worry had gone from her face, to be replaced by a deep annoyance.

'That he was a coward. That he stood by and let them release Sam Bowden, just handed over the keys to the jail. And then had it away on his tail the first chance he got.'

'Is that what they're saying? They should be saying that he stood up to the Bowdens,' Jessie said, snake venom in her voice. 'While the rest of the town hid away.' She wrung her hands together in frustration. 'Cole stood in that street alone against Bowden and his men while the rest of Squaw's good citizens hid away beneath their beds,' she said, speaking slowly and clearly, her fists clenched so that the knuckles shone a bony white. 'This town's full of cowards but Cole Masters ain't one of them.'

'No,' Betty agreed. 'Guess he ain't. All the same he ain't here though.'

'No,' Jessie said. 'He's not.' She had to bite back a wave of emotion that threatened to overwhelm her. It wouldn't do for her to break down in front of the children. She felt a sudden sick feeling in her stomach and knew that wherever Cole was he was facing the gravest danger.

There was, however, one man who could end it all now and that man was Clem Bowden.

The man who carried most of the power in this town.

Jessie looked at Betty and smiled as an insane idea popped into her mind. She had to go and see Clem Bowden, speak to him alone, try to make him see reason. She feared things might have gone too far for that but she had to try. Anything was better than this endless waiting for something to happen.

'Would you do me a favour?' she asked.

'Of course.'

'Will you stay with the children for a few moments?'

Betty seemed taken aback by the request and she looked at the rambunctious children. Her mouth opened but no words came forth. The unexpected request had obviously put her in a flap.

'I'll get them inside,' Jessie said. 'Set them some work and I'll be back before you know it. You won't hear them.'

'Well,' Betty said, 'I've got some chores to do but I suppose it won't hurt for a little while.'

'Thank you,' Jessie said.

'But it will have to be a little while,' Betty said firmly. 'I've got a list as long as my arm of things to take care of.'

'Of course,' Jessie said. 'Thank you again.'

Jessie ran to usher the children into the schoolhouse. They didn't seem at all happy at having their playtime curtailed but when they saw the stern look upon their teacher's face none dared complain. Within minutes she had them all sitting at the desks and had scrawled several sentences on the blackboard for them to copy down.

She introduced Betty as a friend who was going to supervise them while she ran a quick errand.

'I'll be back shortly,' she said in conclusion, and nodded to Betty before leaving the schoolhouse. She hoped the children wouldn't test their mettle against Betty; you had to be stern with them sometimes, their attention tended to wander and they'd misbehave. But she would be quick and now was an opportune time to see Clem Bowden.

Perhaps there wouldn't be another opportunity.

She walked down Main Street with long strides and paused to take a deep breath when she reached the jail-house. For a moment she considered turning back but she steeled herself and knocked upon the door. She didn't wait for an answer before opening the door and walking straight in. Clem Bowden was seated behind the sheriff's desk, Cole's desk, writing in a thick ledger.

'Yes?' He looked up from the book and a puzzled expression crossed his face when he saw Jessie standing there. For a moment he looked troubled, as if expecting the woman to pull a concealed weapon and send him to hell.

'I need to talk to you,' she said.

'Sit down.'

Clem pointed to a chair Jessie had sat in so many times before while visiting Cole. She noticed that Cole's long coat was still hanging on the hook on the far wall and the sight of it made her realize that the old man had no real right to be here at all. This was still Cole's place, always would be as far as she was concerned. There was a freshly printed wanted poster depicting Cole on the wall amongst all the others and she bit her lip to quell her anger.

'What can I do for you?' Clem asked after an awkward silence. He noticed her looking at the wanted poster and smiled, wryly.

'Cole,' Jessie said. 'I want him able to come home. I want this farce to end.'

Again Bowden smiled and said matter of factly: 'Cole Masters killed the sheriff.'

'No,' Jessie shook her head. 'He killed one of your men, and that in a fair fight. Cole is the sheriff.'

Clem Bowden kept his voice level when he spoke but the words might as well have been shouted, such was the power they carried. 'It is true that Steve McCraw once worked for me but he relinquished the position when this town needed a sheriff,' he said. 'And he only wore the star for one day before being gunned down by the cowardly Cole Masters. He was a brave man and didn't deserve to die.'

Jessie had to force herself not to raise her voice. 'Cole was the sheriff,' she said. 'It was you and your men who beat him senseless and then put that interloper in his job. And your rotten son's at the root of all this trouble.'

That seemed to anger the old man and he clenched his fists.

'My son was framed,' he said. 'It was Masters who killed the whore and then framed Sam, who couldn't defend himself in his drunken state. My son can be foolish, granted; high spirits tend to get the better of him, but he's no killer. The law will see that and I've no doubt that Masters will eventually hang for his crimes.'

Jessie shook her head. She realized that there was no pleading with the old man. He was a cold, ruthless son of a bitch. He had worked out his strategy and would stick to it no matter what.

'And the next time your son steps out of line?' Jessie snarled. 'What'll you do then?' She looked deep into Clem Bowden's eyes. 'You're doing him no favours, you know. Covering up for him, cleaning his mess with no consequences on his head. One day he'll do something and you won't be able to get him out of it. Then he'll hang and you'll be responsible.'

Clem Bowden stood up suddenly and reached out, grabbing Jessie by the throat. He pulled his other hand back into a fist and his eyes blazed with fury. He took a deep breath, then gritted his teeth but lowered his fist. 'Tell me,' he said, feigning calmness. 'What do you want me to do?'

Jessie felt a sudden wave of hope. 'Tell the truth,' she said. 'Let your son take his medicine. He'll spend a few years in jail and maybe it'll change him. Maybe he'll become a son you can be proud of. You can't go on covering up for him for the rest of his life.'

Bowden released her and sat back down.

'Cole Masters is guilty of killing that whore,' he said. 'Cole Masters killed the sheriff. And now my son is out there risking his life to bring him to justice.'

'Your son is a dirty cheating liar,' Jessie insisted. Despite being man-handled her blood was boiling and she felt no fear. She no longer saw Clem

Bowden as a threat but more as the pathetic old man he really was. Maybe he actually believed what he was saying, had convinced himself that it was Cole and not his son behind all this. She had seen it all before, parents whose love for their children blinded them to their faults. They would over-indulge the children until they no longer had the power to deny them anything. Children raised in that environment would likely grow up no good.

She was wasting her time here. Clem Bowden had stepped over the line from where there was no return long ago. And Jessie felt he realized it, that he knew his son was a cold, evil man with no positive qualities. He knew it but didn't have the strength to admit it to himself.

'I'd like you to leave now,' Clem said, keeping an even tone of voice. But in his eyes a tornado had been set loose. He seemed to be struggling to keep his fury under control and he had started to twitch beneath his left eye. 'Please leave,' he said, flatly.

'I'm going,' Jessie said. She got up and went to the door. She opened it but before leaving, turned back to Clem Bowden.

'Cole's worth more than you and your son mixed together,' she said. 'And you won't stop him and I tell you here and now, Cole will be back behind that desk long after the Bowden name is forgotten.'

With that she left, slamming the door behind her, and swiftly marched back to the schoolhouse.

16

Cole spotted them first.

'Seems to be just the two men,' Cole said, giving Em a puzzled look.

Em shrugged his shoulders. 'They were all together when I passed them half a day ago.'

There were most definitely only the two riders. They were still some distance off and were only just about recognizable as two mounted men. Cole guessed they were still quite a few miles away. Riding at speed they would reach the mountain range well before sundown. He carefully scanned the horizon, squinting his eyes against the glare, but there was no sign of any other men.

'Do you think they've split up?' Em asked.

'They must have,' Cole said. 'Though I don't see to what purpose. There's no way for a second party to approach without us seeing them. You sure you counted right?'

'My counting was right,' Em insisted. 'There were ten men who left town and the same number earlier.'

'You sure?' Cole asked, remembering the only passage from Shakespeare that had stuck in his mind: *In the night, imagining some fear. How easy the bush is supposed a bear.* He had Sergeant Brannan to thank for his limited cultural knowledge; the big Englishman had quoted the great bard almost daily during the time Cole had served with him in the War Between the States.

'Damn right, I'm sure,' Em said, clearly annoyed. 'I rode all this way to warn you of the posse. I'm not some dude who blows wind.'

'No,' Cole said. If the old man said the posse had been ten strong then that was good enough for him. 'I'm sorry. But where are the others?' he asked presently.

'That's got me in a right bother,' Em said.

'That makes two of us,' Cole said. 'They seem to know where they're heading.'

Em realized that the men's being able to make such good time might be his fault since his trail would be fresh enough to follow without any particular skill. But they would have found Cole in any case; they had followed his track thus far already. They seemed to have the tracking skills only possessed by a few breeds of man — mountain men, scouts, Indians. Still, Em thought, at least he had forewarned Cole.

That gave him a better chance.

Gave them both a better chance.

The two riders looked to be keeping a steady pace as they crossed the grasslands, pushing their horses to the extreme. They still had some distance to come and wouldn't be able to keep it up, they'd have to slow their speed or risk losing their horses. And a man in this country without a horse would find the odds of survival heavily stacked against him.

It would be some time before the riders were close enough to catch a glimpse of them and Cole didn't feel like waiting around for that to happen.

'Come on. Get everything together,' Cole said. He went to the cave entrance and kicked the dirt about a bit, scraping his feet in the mud. He tore off a shred of his shirt and tossed it into the darkness.

'You gone loco?' Em watched him, scratching his head.

'Let's move out,' Cole said, without explaining his actions, and after taking another look at the approaching riders he went and got his bedroll and belongings.

'First we climb up,' Em complained. 'And now you want to go back down. This got me feeling like a child's yo-yo.'

'Afraid so,' Cole said.

He unhitched his horse and started to lead it down into the mountains, Em following closely behind.

'So what's your intention?' Em asked and cursed as he almost stumbled, forcing the roan to pull sharply on its reins. The old man soon regained control and slowly coaxed the horse forward.

'We'll try and avoid them,' Cole said. 'Get away and hope they go up into the mountains looking for us.' He thought of the caves and wondered what the chances were of the two men entering them in their search, hoping they would fall for the little signs he had left in the cave entrance to entice them. If they fell for the lure and got lost he and the old man could be long gone before they found their way out.

It was a long shot but if he, someone who had explored the caves many times previously, could get lost, he was sure these two men, whoever they were, would find themselves fumbling about in darkness for some considerable time.

'I say we hide and shoot the bastards. We could pick them off before they even see us,' Em said. 'Wouldn't need to go up and down these mountains like a pair of cougars, neither.'

Cole grinned coldly but said nothing. The thought had occurred to him but that wasn't his way of doing things. It would be safer and would permanently remove the obstacle from their path but a man had to live with himself.

They continued downwards, entering a flat, tree-lined area. For as long as they could still see the riders they kept descending at more speed than was good for their horses, but as soon as they entered the trees they would lose sight of the riders for perhaps twenty minutes.

The track led down into a valley between two peaks. When they emerged they would be in danger of being spotted by the riders. They had to get down with the utmost care if they were to slip away without the riders noticing them.

'Careful not to skyline yourself,' Cole said. 'Let's get down into the valley and we'll head east for a bit and then come back on ourselves.'

'Still rather fight them,' Em muttered.

'Might come to that,' Cole said and mounted his horse.

The trail had levelled out and gave less difficulty to the horses. It was here that they would make their best time and the more they gained before the men saw them, the better their chances of escaping without the need for a bloody showdown.

Cole thought of the possibility of the other eight men Em had spoken of cutting them off when they got out into the open, trapping them between the two parties. That would make them vulnerable, sitting ducks, but it was a chance they would have to take. Those other men were out there somewhere but he couldn't think about that now. He had to focus on the matter in hand.

17

The descent took longer than they had expected.

This was largely because Em's horse seemed to be terrified of the steeper sections of the mountain and took some considerable coaxing to move. Eventually though, they made it.

'Where now?' Em asked, panting from exertion. The climb down had, if anything, been worse than going up. His legs ached, his back ached, his arms ached — in fact if there was a part of his body that didn't ache then he couldn't locate it.

'They can't be far off,' Cole said.

There was no sign of them at the moment, but they didn't have the view they'd had up in the mountains. There was a trail to the east that led them amongst the tall pines and rolling hills. They'd be able to remain hidden and get far enough away to turn back towards Squaw unnoticed, crossing the river upstream of the rapids.

The only problem with the plan was that Cole had no idea where the rest of the posse were and he feared riding straight into them.

'Then let's get moving,' Em said. 'If you're going to hang around for a fight then we should have done so back up there.' He motioned back the way they had come.

'You've lost your bloodlust?'

'Hell no,' Em retorted. 'But coming down here takes away our best advantage.'

'Then let's ride.' Cole said. 'And try and keep that horse of yours under control.'

'She don't like heights is all,' Em said.

Cole chuckled and spurred his horse onwards, leading the way into the thicket and the forest beyond. They rode for a few hundred yards and then once again had to go on foot to lead the horses down a steep incline.

Eventually after much cursing and coaxing the horses they reached the foot of the mountains. They led the horses off into the trees and rode them for perhaps half a mile before Cole pulled his horse to a stop.

'We'll tether the horses here,' Cole said. 'Walk back a ways and watch the posse approach. Make sure they go up into the mountains.'

Em nodded. It seemed like a prudent idea to him. If they had managed to shake the two riders off their tail it made sense to know one way or the other. And from what he had seen of the two men shaking them off was anything but a sure thing. Those men stuck to them like cheap whores to paid-up cowboys.

He checked his rifle and dismounted.

On foot, they made their way back through the thicket, and climbed the banking that had proved so troublesome for the horses. Once on top, which offered them a good view, towards the mountains, they saw the two riders. They were not more than a couple of thousand feet away, almost within earshot.

Lying in the long grass Cole watched as the two men stood beside their horses and seemed to be contemplating which way to go. He didn't like the look of them. Em had been right — these men were both professional killers. They each had rifles in their saddle boots and wore long trail coats.

Cole could see that one of them was indeed a half-breed, with either Indian or Mexican blood running through his veins. Even from this distance he looked impressive. Long jet black hair hung from the sides of his hat and framed a cruel looking set of features.

'What they doing?' Em whispered.

'Beats me,' Cole said.

He tried to make out the men's features but they were too far away. He could just make out the dark complexion of the taller of the two and his long black hair, brushed back and hanging in a tail from the back of his Stetson.

Cole felt there was something familiar about him, as though he knew him from sometime back. He tried to recall but the memory wouldn't come; he had such a lot of life to sift through and for the moment it escaped him.

'Come on, come on,' Em whispered as he watched the two men. They seemed to be considering which trail to take up into the mountains.

'Don't look good,' Cole said and froze as the taller of the two men turned and looked in their direction.

Cole felt his heart miss a beat and for one awful moment he felt that the man had seen them and that his eyes had burned into his soul. But then the man turned away and knelt to examine the ground.

'He knows,' Em said. 'He knows we ain't even up there.'

'We didn't have time to wipe our tracks,' Cole said. He shared the old man's anguish but the eternal optimist inside him was hoping the two men would suddenly develop myopia.

It was looking more and more as though the men had not been fooled and wouldn't bother going up into the mountains in search of them.

Cole clenched his fists and prayed silently beneath his breath.

Em cocked his rifle, sending a bullet into the breech. He was about to take aim, ready to fire as soon as the men came into range. If the man came towards them Em figured on taking at least one of them out before they knew what was happening, but Cole motioned to lower the rifle.

With a frown Em did so.

'Move back quietly but quickly,' Cole said. 'Let's get out of here. Let's put some distance between us.'

'I think they'll follow,' Em said.

'Maybe,' Cole replied. 'That's a chance we'll have to take.'

He took another look at the men. They appeared to be deep in conversation, seemingly discussing the route to take up into the mountains. Who were these men?

Cole and Em slid backwards, then moved down the banking and went into the thicket. They moved as quickly as they could back to their horses, but took care not to make too much sound. It was unlikely that the men would hear them but neither wanted to chance it.

They reached their horses and mounted up. Then, after a quick glance over his shoulder, Cole set the pace and took his horse forward at a steady trot. He wanted to get some more distance between them and the men before gaining speed.

The sound of a galloping horse could travel a fair way in country like this.

'Guess we lost them after all,' Em said, looking back.

They had covered perhaps a mile and there was no sign of the men behind them. Thinking the men must have gone up in the mountains after all, the old man started to feel a little easier. He patted the roan's neck.

'Now we just got to worry about coming across the others,' Cole said.

Em nodded. 'Sure is curious them two being alone. Maybe they scouted on ahead and left the others at their camp.'

Cole had already considered that but it didn't seem likely. 'Can't see no sense in that,' he said.

'I think the most deadly ones are the two we just left behind in any case,' Em said. 'Sam Bowden's nothing to fear and the rest of them are hired hands. Cowboys, nothing more. Doubt if many of them could shoot any straighter than a temperance woman with eye-glasses.'

'Still pays to be cautious.' Cole took his tobacco from his saddlebags and grabbed his pipe out of his shirt. He thumbed the Durham into the bowl and brought a match to the pipe.

Cole figured they needed to travel another ten miles before crossing the river and setting camp for the night. They'd need to be on the move again just after first light if they were to meet the stage before it got to Squaw. There was still enough time to ride straight into trouble if they didn't take care.

Cole knew he'd be fine to ride through the night but he wasn't too sure of Em. The old man had already had a hard ride getting here and although he'd not complained the pace must have been taking its toll on him. And of course stumbling about after dark would be a sure way to walk right into the rest of the posse. No, travelling after dark was not really an option.

'It'll all be over soon enough,' Cole said.

'Amen to that,' Em said and then added with a toothless grin: 'Let's hope we're alive to see it.'

'Can't even think otherwise,' Cole said. 'I've gone too far with this thing to take a bullet now.'

'Going into town with the stage is just as likely to get you killed,' Em pointed out.

'No.' Cole shook his head and puffed hard at his pipe to remove a piece of tobacco that was blocking the stem. 'As soon as Clem Bowden sees the judge he'll have to end it all. He'll have to let his son take his chances against the law. Clem Bowden's an evil son of a bitch but he's no fool.'

'His son's sheriff,' Em reminded him. 'That might carry some weight with the judge.'

'The judge will see through all that,' Cole said. 'I think he'll believe my story. As long as I get to him before Clem has a chance to sully the water. And I'm banking on a few of the townsfolk speaking up once they see the way things are going.'

'Not much hope of them cowards speaking,' Em said. 'It'd be more likely for the Lord to swoop down and take out the Bowdens himself.'

'We'll see,' Cole said. 'We'll see.' He puffed on the pipe and then speeded the horse up slightly, feeling less on edge now.

'Don't matter,' Em said. 'First we got to get away from this darned posse. Everything else will have to take its course.'

'So far so good,' Cole said and then

wished he hadn't as he heard the sound of galloping horses behind them.

They looked at each other in stunned disbelief and then behind them. They both turned in the saddle and then looked at each other again.

Sure enough the riders were coming, horses galloping like the wind.

'Shit,' Em said and let off a wild shot at the men. Not aimed, fired from the back of a moving horse, the bullet went all to hell.

The two men ignored the shot and kept coming at the same relentless speed.

'Who are these men?' Cole asked as he kicked his own horse into a gallop.

18

They were gaining on them and Cole chanced a shot.

He knew he had little chance of hitting them but he was hoping to slow them down, send them scrambling for cover. Even a split second gained meant all the difference, but the shot went far wide and the men continued to come without the slightest pause.

Cole tried to coax more speed out of his horse and he looked across at Em on the old roan. He was keeping up thus far but the horse would soon run out of steam and he wouldn't be able to ride on without the old man. There was no other thing for it, there was no longer any choice in the matter. They would have to stop and make a fight of it. Cole cursed his decision to leave the mountains. Maybe he should have stayed put and picked the men off as they approached. It was academic now since very soon the men would be upon them.

Then it would become a very simple case of fight or die.

'Not too far ahead,' Cole shouted, 'there's some cover. We'll stand and fight there.'

Em waved a hand to say he understood and went about the difficult task of keeping himself upon his galloping horse. The wind hit his face and lifted his hat from his head, sending it spinning off into the air behind them.

They rounded a corner and Cole's horse almost stumbled but managed to regain its balance without toppling itself or its rider. Again Cole let off a wild shot behind him. The riders were now in range and gaining on them, slowing them down for even a split second mattered more than ever. They needed to get enough time to get under cover before fighting the riders.

'Come on,' Cole yelled and spurred

his horse harder than he ever had before which did little to gain more speed. 'The next corner,' he yelled. 'Get down behind whatever cover you can find.'

'Sure,' Em shouted and felt his stomach lurch as the roan somehow picked up more speed and nosed in front of Cole's far superior stallion.

'That damn horse's possessed,' Cole called after him, but he wasn't sure if the old man had heard him.

Suddenly Cole pulled his horse to a sudden stop and turned, firing both Colts, while the old man dismounted and placed himself behind a large rock. That slowed the two riders and Cole used the opportunity to get behind a rock himself and reload his weapons. He looked to his left and saw Em was already up, firing his rifle at the men, causing them to dive for cover themselves.

Em whooped in delight. 'Come on you varmints,' he yelled. 'Pop those heads up and I'll fire them clean off.'

'Wait till you've got a clear target to

shoot,' Cole warned. He peered out from behind the rock but had to duck back down immediately when a bullet struck the rock barely inches from his face. He saw sparks and heard it whine off harmlessly into the undergrowth.

That had been too close for comfort.

Suddenly both of their pursuers stood up at once and fired their rifles. Neither Cole nor Em realized what was happening, as the shots seemed to travel wide of both of them. They kept their heads down while the furious onslaught of lead continued. The two men seemed to be wasting their ammunition and hoping for a lucky hit but when Cole turned he saw that the men had indeed hit what they had been aiming for. The cold, calculating bastards.

Cole's horse had taken a bullet in the neck and it was jumping about wildly, pulling at its reins while blood turned its thick coat a sickening black. Em's horse was down on the ground, dead, having taken a remarkably aimed shot right between the eyes. It would have died instantly and not known what had hit it. The other horse wasn't so fortunate and it kicked and bucked in pain.

'Bastards,' Em shouted and stood up, sending lead every which way. 'You killed my horse, you bastards.'

Cole had to break cover and dive onto the old man, pinning him to the ground. He lay there and watched his own horse weaken from the blood loss and slump down on its front legs. It was a pitiful sight and the horse's eyes seemed to be imploring its owner to help as its life force drained from it. Cole would have shot it, finished it off but he couldn't afford the ammunition. Not the way things were going.

'They killed my horse,' Em protested. 'What did they want to go and do that for?'

They both knew why they had taken the horses out, though. They had cut them off, there was no escape, and the men seemed confident that they would prove victorious in this fight. At the moment it was stalemate — neither side could make a move without the other gunning them down. The two men might have all the time in the world, be able to wait this out, but Cole didn't.

Now there was no doubt, if indeed there ever had been, that these men were professional killers. They operated with the cold efficiency of men used to killing, men who had much experience with guns and felt no emotion whether gunning down man or animal.

'Keep your head,' Cole said. 'These men will make the best of any chance they get.'

'Bastards,' Em said, looking back at the fallen roan. He wiped the back of his hand across his face and seemed close to breaking down. 'I'll get them, girl,' he said to the fallen horse. 'Don't you worry any about that.'

Cole shook his head and turned to peer out from the side of the rock but both men were lying there, rifles sighted in their direction, patiently waiting for a clear shot. They were not about to make any reckless moves and seemed content to wait them out.

They weren't going to waste any ammunition.

'Who are you?' Cole shouted, thinking that building up a dialogue was the best chance he had until an opportunity to put a slug into either of the men presented itself.

Cole's words were greeted with silence though, and he shouted again: 'What do you want?'

Again nothing but silence.

'Answer him, you cowardly horse killers,' Em shouted.

Again silence but then one of the men spoke up.

'We want you, Masters.'

'Do I know you?' Cole shouted back and shrugged his shoulders. He considered jumping up, trying to take them by surprise but decided against it. These men were expert shots. There were times when suddenly rushing an opponent was a good strategy but this was not one of those times.

'We want Cole Masters for the brutal murder of the sheriff of Squaw.' It was the same voice, a cold guttural drawl.

'Who are you?' Cole shouted, frantically trying to think of something, anything that would help their situation. He noticed that his own horse now lay still on the ground, not quite dead, its breathing was ragged, but not too far off. Before long it would be out of its pain for ever.

'You working for Clem Bowden?' Cole shouted back as his eyes scanned their surroundings. There was little cover each side of them and to move they had to go out in to the open, which was not really an option.

'We've been deputized by the sheriff,' came the reply. Again it was the same voice while the other man remained silent.

'Sam Bowden,' Cole yelled, 'is a worthless piece of horse-shit.'

'That's as maybe,' came the reply. 'But he wears the badge of office. Makes him the sheriff no matter what

203

kind of man he is.'

'Who are you?' Cole yelled back. He tried to peer around the rock to see if he had a clear shot but both men were hidden behind the bank. Only the muzzles of their rifles were visible.

'Names don't matter.'

'To hell they don't,' Cole said. He jumped up and let off three shots before ducking back behind the rock and crouching while a hail of gunfire sent sparks from the rock.

Cole had been hoping for a lucky shot, to catch one of them before they could react, but it was no surprise when it didn't work. It had been the slimmest of slim chances in any case, so the outcome was no surprise to either of them. He supposed he should consider himself lucky that he had made it back behind the cover of the rock without getting his own fool head blown off.

'That's sure waiting for a target,' Em said and took a shot himself.

He spun around and fired from the side of the rock but his bullet spat up soil as it buried itself into the ground.

It was a stalemate and all there was to do was for each side to wait the other out. Cole was aware that this situation could go on indefinitely. The two gunmen would no doubt have the patience to sit it out but he didn't have time to waste. And now that they were without horses escape, even if it was possible, was not an option. Things had to be brought to a head.

They had to either kill or incapacitate the men and take their horses. Cole guessed the former since men such as these would go down figting.

'They should hang folk for killing horses like that,' Em said. He kept glancing at the roan. Cole's horse lay beside it and it was clear that it too had died. 'Bastard,' he muttered under his breath.

'We've got to get out of here,' Cole said.

'Any ideas?'

'Other than running and hoping for the best,' Cole said with a wry smile, 'no. None.'

'What do you think of our chances of rushing them?' Em asked. He had been in similar situations to this before and the tactic, risky as it was, did often work. Trouble was, when it didn't the results were usually fatal.

'I've already considered that and there's no chance,' Cole said. 'I'd prefer it if they tried to rush us.'

'Which they won't.'

'No,' Cole agreed. 'And for the same reasons as we won't try it on them.'

Cole recoiled as a bullet tore into the ground only inches from his left boot. He rolled on his stomach and shot back but again there was no target to hit.

'You shoot,' Em said. 'And get back down quickly. As soon as one of them comes up to fire back I'll get him.' The old man slid across to the edge of the large rock and peered around it. 'I've got a clear sight on where they are. Just need them to pop their heads up.'

Cole nodded and reloaded both of his pistols.

Cole said a silent prayer and made

the sign of the cross before leaping and firing several shots from each of the Colts. He saw one of the men come up for a shot back and then he saw the man double up as Em's Spencer struck home.

'Boyd!' The other gunman shouted out like a wild animal, a blood-chilling wail and broke cover himself, swinging the evil eye of his rifle towards the old man. He pumped the action like a madman, sending red-hot lead scream-ing towards Em.

'I've got him!' Em shouted. 'I've got the son of a bitch.'

Em moved back towards the rock but he was careless in his elation and he was spun around as Quill sent a slug into his leg. Em yelled in pain and reached for the leg but another bullet found his stomach, lifting him and hurling him backwards as the bullet tore through his internal organs. He hit the ground hard, blood seeping from between his fingers as he clutched at the gut wound.

'I've been shot,' Em groaned and looked down at his wound. At that moment he knew that he was already dead and that all that remained was the dying. 'I've been killed.'

'No,' Cole shouted and broke cover, running to the old man. He saw the remaining gunman pop up and sight his rifle. Almost immediately a bullet whistled past his ear and Cole fired back from both Colts, diving as he did so. He came down hard on the ground beside the old man and he fired again. This time luck was with him and he couldn't have found his target more true had he taken all day about aiming.

The gunman had been standing, taking careful aim with his rifle, but his finger had hesitated too long on the trigger and Cole's lucky shot went clean between his eyes. His arms threw wide and for a moment he stood there, staring through blood-filled eyes, a stunned expression on his face, as if unable to believe that he had been hit, before swaying on his feet and then falling forward onto the ground.

'Em,' Cole said and knelt over the old man. There was a huge gaping wound in his stomach and gore seeped through it and was mixing with the blood and dirt on the ground.

All colour had drained from the old man's face and he looked ghastly. His eyes were dreadfully bloodshot and blood trickled from the corners of his mouth. His breathing was shallow, blood bubbled in the back of his throat, threatening to choke him

'Did I kill him?' Em asked, coughing as his mouth filled with thick blood that dribbled down his chin. He winced in pain with each breath and his mind started to cloud over. The world seemed to darken as if nightfall had come early.

'You killed him,' Cole said. 'Between us we got them both.'

'They killed me too,' Em said. He coughed again and blood bubbled from his mouth. 'Guess I'm gonna ride that roan again after all,' he said. Then his eyes rolled back in their sockets as he breathed his last breath.

Em Tanner was dead.

For a long while Cole knelt there, beside the old man. His head bowed, he closed his eyes and felt a wave of mixed emotions — regret, grief, guilt but above all a seething anger.

Eventually Cole stood up and went over to the fallen gunmen. Mechanically he removed their weapons from their corpses and then went and got one of their horses. The other horse he tethered to the gnarled branch of a long-dead tree.

He took a bedroll from the saddle and used it to create a makeshift shroud for Em. He tied it around the old man's body and then lifted him and carefully placed the body over the horse. Next he collected both his own and Em's belongings from their dead horses and tied them next to the old man. He kept the Winchester and slid it into the boot of the other horse.

Then and only then did he walk over and take a look at the two gunmen. Em had been right: the first man was definitely of mixed race, a half-breed with his Indian side being genetically dominant. The other man, the one Em's rifle had made short work of, was white. He lay there, a ghastly sight, his eyes wide open and sightless in death with a third bloody eye between them.

Cole searched the bodies for any evidence to link the men with Clem Bowden but all he found was a thick envelope which contained $1,000. Blood money, more than likely. He put the money into his own saddlebag, thinking that the cash would, if not tie the men to Bowden, at least add weight to the charge that he had hired them.

Scum, Cole thought.

'Ain't wasting time burying you,' Cole said without looking back at the two men. 'Buzzards got to eat.'

Cole reached into his shirt and removed the buckled badge. With his thumb he wiped at the bloodstain, Steve McCaw's blood, and then pinned the badge on.

He was still the sheriff of Squaw and he was going to stop the stage, and bring the Bowdens, both of the sons of bitches, to justice. Too many men had died here today and one of them at least had been a good man; a damn good man.

Maybe there would be other deaths before this was all over but that was the way it had to be. It was Bowden who had forced things this way and by God he was going to pay.

Cole mounted up and sent the large horse trotting forward. He had the reins of the horse carrying Em tied to his saddle horn, and the horse followed behind at the casual pace Cole set.

'It ends now,' Cole said and bit back a tear at Em's passing.

There would be time enough for grieving later.

For now the only emotion he needed was the seething anger in the pit of his stomach, for it would keep him fresh, help him remain focused on what had to be done.

He looked down at the buckled badge

he wore and it became more than what it actually was to him. He saw it as a symbol of all things right and a harbinger of destruction to all that stood against it. It represented a law higher than that of man; it was a weapon in the eternal battle between good and evil.

Cole thumbed tobacco into his pipe and took a match to it. He smoked slowly and rode even more slowly, all the while his every limb ready to spring into action should he come across the remainder of the posse. But the journey went without event and soon, after crossing the river, Cole saw the trail the missing posse members had left as they'd ridden off, back towards the town of Squaw.

That was one mystery solved and Cole looked back at Em's body, draped in the makeshift shroud and tied over the horse. 'Guess you were right, old man,' he said and then spurred the horse to gain a little speed.

The sheriff of Squaw rode on, his mind set on the final showdown.

19

Cole eased his horse forward and looked down onto the landscape below him. The stage was nowhere to be seen but he knew it would be approaching soon. He filled his pipe with the last of his tobacco and smoked while he waited.

He figured he had less than an hour to wait before the stage showed up on the horizon. It would have reached the fort the previous night and was due to leave for Squaw at daybreak. Sam Bowden's trial had been scheduled for this coming Monday and the judge would be expecting things to go ahead as planned.

As far as was possible, that was still Cole's intention.

Earlier Cole had tethered the horse carrying Em's body to a tree. He'd collect it later, after squaring things with the judge, and take the old man into Squaw for burial. He had considered burying him out here in the wilderness, amongst the landscape over which the old man had wandered so many times in his younger days, but he preferred to give him his final resting place close by.

The grave would be easier to tend that way and Cole planned on taking care of the old man's plot. When this was all over he'd visit with Jessie and together they would make sure there were always fresh flowers to mark his spot.

He figured it was the least he could do seeing that he owed the old-timer his life.

Throwing caution to the wind, Cole had ridden through the night, all the while alert for the remaining members of the posse, but the ride had passed without event. They must have long reached Squaw and would not be expecting him to return.

He was looking forward to showing

them that they were wrong.

He sat there, upon the bluff, looking down on a landscape that was both beautiful and challenging, and waited for the stage. He smoked the pipe until it went out and suddenly felt bone-tired; recent events were catching up with him, and there was no part of his body that didn't seem to throb. The bruising of his beating at the hands of Bowden's foreman had all but healed, but the pain he felt now was not due to any physical injury.

It was a mixture of exhaustion and grief and it sprang from the centre of his very being.

* * *

'You really are a stupid son of a bitch,' Clem Bowden said and shook his head in disappointment. 'Don't you ever listen, boy?'

'Goddamn it. They were leading us ragged,' Sam protested.

He was weary from the long ride and

216

all he wanted now was a drink and then a long uninterrupted period in bed. 'They weren't going to find Masters. They went off his trail and led us clean across country. Enough was enough.'

Clem Bowden looked at his son as he had so many times before, a look of distaste in his eyes. He wanted to tell him that those two men were the best trackers in the territory, that they could do things with a gun that would leave him standing, that they were worth twice, no, ten times what he was, but instead he said nothing and merely shook his head.

The expression upon his face and his sad, sunken eyes spoke volumes, though.

'Cole Masters is long gone,' Sam continued. 'Now let's leave it at that.' Again Clem ignored his son and looked at the rest of the men.

They were all weary and trail dust clung to them like an outer skin. They were good men, all things considered, and Clem knew it wasn't their fault that they had broken away from Quill and

Boyd. They would have been confused, unsure whom to take orders from, and their loyalties to him would have made them side with his son. Couldn't really blame them for that but the problem was, his son was a buffoon.

Clem considered keeping them in town but decided against it. The posse was too worn out to be of any use to him and he already had a half-dozen of his best men stationed in town. If Cole had managed to elude the two manhunters and made it back to Squaw, then he had all the protection he needed already here in place. These men needed food, rest and a clean-up before they would be of any use either to themselves or to anyone else.

'You men,' he said, 'go back to the ranch. Get yourselves rested up.'

Without another word the riders turned and wearily headed back out of town, leaving the old man standing there in the street with his son. After a few moments of silence Clem turned to his son and the look of disappointment on his face showed more clearly than ever.

He seemed to regard his son the way one looked at a diseased range dog.

'Pa?' Sam gave the old man a quizzical look. He didn't like what he saw in his father's eyes and at that moment he felt something happen between them that he couldn't really understand. He felt a strange sensation of expanding space between them and he realized that when this was all over things would never again be the same.

'What do you want me to do now?' he asked, not liking the uncomfortable feeling between them.

'You're the sheriff,' Clem snapped. 'Get over the hotel and get yourself washed up and then get back here.'

'Thought maybe I'd get some sleep,' Sam said. 'I'm bushed.'

'You're the sheriff,' Clem repeated with a sigh. 'The stage'll be here just after noon with the judge on board. He's come here to sit over your trial so I suppose you should be here to explain the situation. When he arrives I want you there to meet him. You can sleep later if you're not back in the jailhouse.'

'Yes sir,' Sam said, but he cursed the old man beneath his breath.

He was a grown man and, as his father had said, the sheriff of this sorry excuse for a town. He guessed he could pretty much do what he wanted and right now he had a burning desire for a strong drink and maybe a woman before sleeping off the effects of the past few days.

There was no use arguing with the old man, though, and he guessed there would be time enough for pleasures later.

Clem Bowden opened the door of the jailhouse but before entering he turned back and took another lingering look at his son. 'And stay out of the saloon.' How well the man knew the boy. With that he went inside and slammed the door behind him.

Sam stood there for several long minutes, an anger seething up inside him that threatened to take all reason from him. He had to resist the urge to burst into the jail-house there and then and put a bullet into the miserable old bastard he called his father. These thoughts were not new but it used to be that he felt ashamed and would suppress them. Now he would like nothing better than to act upon them.

He spat into the dust. 'One day,' he mumbled, then turned and walked away from the jailhouse. He kept his head bowed to the ground as he walked and ignored the sensation of feeling as though he was being watched.

* * *

Across the street Jessie watched the exchange between the two men.

Today being Saturday, not a school day, she had been tending to her garden, anything to take her mind off things, when the posse had ridden in to town.

She crouched lower down behind the

picket fence Cole had built for her as Sam Bowden turned and walked over to the Rainbow Hotel.

She wondered what had happened. Where were the two men who had led the posse? What had happened to Cole and Em? She didn't think the posse had caught up with them and although she couldn't hear what words had been spoken across the street it was obvious from the men's manner that their mission had not been a success.

She stood up and looked up and down Main Street. Now that Sam Bowden had gone into the hotel and his father to the jailhouse, the street was deserted. It should have been bustling, even this early on a Saturday morning, but there was a feeling of foreboding that hung like a dark cloud over the town and kept the citizens off the street for all but the most important of chores.

Even the Majestic, usually a hive of sin, seemed quiet and there was none of the usual laughter or music drifting through its batwings.

The town of Squaw was in terminal decline and she knew that it would continue to wither away until nothing remained. The town had a cancer, a powerful malignant tumour that gnawed away at its heart and soul and unless it was cut away there could be no hope.

That cancer went by the name of Bowden.

* * *

Cole had been napping, sitting on his horse, when he heard a faint rumble. He looked, squinting against the sun, and in the distance he saw the tiny speck that he knew was the stage. He scanned the landscape for the remainder of the posse but still they were nowhere to be seen.

He took a drink of water from his canteen and spurred his horse forward, taking it slowly as they made their way down the hill to the flatland below.

He checked his Colts and the

Winchester and then made sure that his badge was visible on his chest. Once again he turned the events of the last few days over in his mind, wanting to get everything clear before he spoke to the judge.

No doubt the Bowdens would contest his story but he hoped his reputation as an honest man, a brave man, a good and courageous sheriff would add a little extra clout to his words. And maybe if the townsfolk saw the way things were going they would stand up and speak out. Bowden ruled the town by fear and Cole knew that was always a tenuous grip. Once broken the Bowden empire would crumble like a sand-fort in the wind. Fear never made a solid foundation for anything worth while. It only took one man to stand up and confront it head on and the shackles it imposed would fall away. Folk would suddenly find the strength to stand up and speak out against their former masters.

Cole steadied his horse and sat there

in the road like some highwayman as the stage approached. All the while he was alert for any riders; he feared Bowden's men would turn up at any moment and attempt to finish him off there and then.

He wasn't going to let that happen.

Not after all that had happened.

He sat and waited.

As the stage neared, he raised his empty hands toward the sky to show he had peaceful intent and shouted for the stage to stop. The driver and the man beside him riding shotgun exchanged puzzled looks but pulled the stage to a perfect halt.

'I'm Sheriff Cole Masters of Squaw,' Cole said. 'Have you got the judge on board?'

'We have,' answered the driver, a short podgy man with skin that had been burnt bronze over years of exposure to the elements.

'I need to speak with him,' Cole said. He dismounted and walked towards the stage.

20

Cole rode into Squaw ahead of the coach, trailing the horse carrying Em's body behind him, and made straight for the jailhouse.

He saw Jessie out of the corner of one eye; she had seen him too and was running towards him, a mixture of relief and horror on her face.

Cole raised a hand, warning her to stay away, to go back to the house. She took his meaning correctly and after glancing at the shrouded body on the back of the horse she turned and headed back to her place.

Cole dismounted outside the jailhouse and hitched both horses to the rail. He slid the Winchester from the boot and stood there in the street. He looked up and down Main Street but there was no one to be seen. He turned and walked over to the general store, where he tucked himself away in the alley between it and the livery stable.

He waited for the stage, which was only a few minutes behind him, all the while keeping his eyes on the street. But for the moment everything was silent.

When he had stopped the coach earlier he had told the judge everything that had occurred over these last few days; it seemed like years since he had taken the beating in Main Street. Cole had told the judge everything, leaving nothing out, going all the way back to the killing of the whore. And to his surprise the judge had insisted on continuing to Squaw and assisting in Cole's arrest of the Bowden faction, as he called it. There would be no need for military intervention as the judge was confident he could deal with the Bowdens. From the way Cole had described them, the judge felt they would buckle when they saw the weight of the law against them. It was one thing disputing Cole's word but they would never go against a territorial judge. The truth will out, the judge had said.

The one compromise Cole had won was that he would ride in ahead of the stage, make sure the coast was clear. And so, after collecting Em's body, that was what he had done.

Cole heard the coach approaching. Then, seconds later, it came into Main Street, the six-strong team slowing to a gentle trot. The coach pulled to a stop in the centre of the street, the jailhouse opened and both Clem and Sam Bowden emerged. They looked down at the horses tethered at the rail, then Sam Bowden went and pulled the shroud from the body. He stood back when he recognized the old man.

'It's old man Tanner!' he exclaimed and looked at his father, a vacant expression on his face.

'I can see that,' Clem said. He recognized the horses as being those of Quill and Boyd but the gunmen were nowhere to be seen. A puzzled expression crossed his face.

He looked at the stage and watched as the door was opened and a small portly man stepped out into the street. Out of the corner of his eye Clem saw a number of his men emerge from the saloon and take up positions in the street while they waited for an order from their boss.

'I'm Judge Lucas Meredith.' The small man introduced himself and smiled his thanks when one of the stage drivers handed him his bag. 'I'm looking for the sheriff.'

'That'll be me,' Sam Bowden said and stepped down off the boardwalk.

'No,' Cole said, stepping out into the open, his rifle cocked and ready to fire with the butt resting against his hip. 'That'll be me.'

The judge didn't flinch and it was obvious to Clem Bowden that Masters had briefed him and that he knew what was going on. The expression on his face was one of solid, fearless resolve.

The street now was filling with onlookers and for the first time in a long while Clem Bowden felt that things had moved beyond his control.

It was not a feeling he liked.

'Masters.' Sam Bowden looked first at his father and then at Cole. He seemed to be at a loss as to what to do next and his hands hovered dangerously close to his side arms. He felt the first tinge of fear as he looked into Cole Masters's eyes and then noticed the buckled tin star he wore.

Clem Bowden stepped down off the boardwalk and went and stood in front of his son. He looked first at the judge and then at Masters and for the first time in his life he knew what it was like to truly feel threatened.

This really wasn't going the way he had planned it.

'I'm Clem Bowden,' he said and held out a hand to the judge, but the gesture was refused and the judge looked through him towards Cole.

'You'll find what's left of your two gunmen back on Squaw Mountain,' Cole said. 'They were responsible for that.' He pointed with his rifle at Em's body, his face revealed where Sam had pulled the shroud aside.

Em's ghastly lifeless eyes seemed to be watching things unfold, mocking the Bowdens from beyond the grave.

Clem turned. He took a long lingering look at the body and then he shook his head. 'I don't know any gunmen,' he said with a faint smile. 'I'm an honest businessman and my son's the sheriff of this town.'

'Your son's a lying cheating killer,' Cole said. 'And that man there,' again he motioned towards Em's body, 'was killed by a gunman who was in your employ. That makes you responsible. You're as guilty as the man who pulled the trigger.' He carefully reached into his shirt and removed the envelope containing the money. He tossed it into the street. 'There's the money you paid them.'

'Nonsense — ' Clem started, but his words were cut dead by Cole talking over him.

231

'I'm arresting you both,' Cole said. 'You'll both face trial for murder.'

'She was just a goddamn whore,' Sam shouted and ignored his father who was trying to silence him before he said anything more damning. 'All this over a cheap whore who was of no account to anyone in any case.'

'Shut up,' Clem Bowden snapped but he knew that enough had already been said. If the judge wasn't siding with Cole already, and he certainly appeared to be doing so, then this latest outburst had sealed the deal. It was obvious the judge had already accepted the truth of whatever turn of events Cole had told him and now his damn fool son had given all the evidence they needed to convict them both.

His son as a killer and he himself as an accessory after the fact.

'No, I won't shut up,' Sam said and drew his Colt. He stepped backwards a few paces and held the gun covering both his father and Cole. 'I'm sick and tired of being told to shut up. Well, for once you can shut up, old man.'

'Put the gun down,' Cole said. He could see Bowden's men run onto the street, weapons drawn but confused as to where to aim now that the son was threatening the father.

People ran every which way looking for cover and Cole indicated with his eyes for the judge to do likewise. The judge seemed to understand. Silently he edged over towards the livery stable, then vanished into the alleyway.

'I'm through taking orders from anyone,' Sam Bowden said. 'And that includes you, Masters.'

'It's over,' Cole told him. 'You shoot now and your father won't be able to buy you out of trouble. Put the gun down and let's end this peaceable.'

'Listen to him.' Clem Bowden looked at his son with thunder in his face. His eyes were squinted tight and his mouth was pulled back into a grim scowl. 'Drop the gun and don't say anything else. We'll let our lawyers handle this.'

'Ain't no fancy lawyer going to save

you, old man.' Cole smiled at Clem Bowden as he spoke. 'You hired those killers who did for my best friend. You're going to pay for that.'

'I don't know anything about any men, killers or otherwise,' Clem Bowden insisted, speaking as cool as you like.

Cole had to give it to the elder Bowden. When it came to deviousness he was as good as they came and could certainly keep his head in a crisis. He looked around the street and counted seven of Bowden's men, all armed. They stood there, not believing what was unfolding before their eyes.

Cole wasn't sure whether the old man was armed but there were at least eight guns to contend with here. He was hoping that if he disarmed Sam the old man would keep his men at a distance and take his chances with the law. His kind was arrogant enough to think his money could buy them out of any situation.

Well, that wasn't going to be the case this time.

The situation was remarkably similar to the one Cole had found himself in only a few days ago, when Clem Bowden had ridden into town with the intention of releasing his son. The only difference was that this time the Bowdens had turned against each other.

That could make it all the more dangerous.

Cole looked at the star on his chest and made a silent vow that one way or another he was going to stand his ground.

'This is your last warning,' he said. 'Drop the weapon. I intend to arrest you.'

'Sam,' Clem Bowden said firmly. 'Drop the gun this instant.'

'No,' Sam yelled defiantly and fired.

The bullet took Clem Bowden in the chest but somehow the old man remained standing. He stared at his son with disbelief in his eyes. He shook his head, then Sam fired again, blowing a hole in his father's gut and sending him punching back against the wall where he slid, dead, to the ground.

Sam Bowden took advantage of the confusion and unhitched the horse Cole had ridden in on from the rail. He jumped onto it and fired in Cole's direction, forcing the sheriff to duck into the alleyway. Then he galloped along the street and headed out of town.

Cole came out of the alleyway and saw Sam disappear around the corner. He ran to old man Bowden and bent down to him, but he was already dead. He lay there, eyes open, staring towards a heaven he had no chance of entering. His men crowded around the sheriff and the body of their boss and not a single one of them made any move to fight.

'Get him over to the undertaker's,' Cole said. 'I need a horse.'

'Take mine from the livery stable,' the late Clem Bowden's new foreman said. 'The white pony.'

'Thanks,' Cole said. He noticed the

judge standing in the street, watching the mêlée with a look of horror upon his face.

Cole went to him and led him across the street to Jessie's place, where he introduced him to the schoolteacher, requesting her to look after him. Then he left town in pursuit of Sam Bowden.

21

Cole heard the gunshot and instinctively rolled sideways in the saddle. Pulling his horse to a sudden stop, he let himself fall. He hit the ground hard and came up in a crouch, weapon drawn and ready to fire. He used the cover of his horse running off to scramble behind a bank, where he sat, holding the gun at the ready, while he caught his breath.

Another shot. The bullet hit the bank and struck a stone before whistling off into thin air.

Cole shot back without any clear target, then peered over the bank. He could see Bowden, standing upon another bank that ran alongside an irrigation ditch. He fired again but missed and the bullet spat earth at Sam Bowden.

Cole ducked back down just as a bullet whizzed past his head.

It had been close.

For a moment there was perfect silence while both men waited for the other to make a move; then Sam Bowden shouted: 'I killed my father.'

'You did,' Cole answered.

'It's your fault.'

'No,' Cole said. 'You can't even take responsibility for that. You're a sorry excuse for a man and an even worse example of a son. Your father went to the grave knowing what a waste of good air you are.'

'Bastard,' Sam Bowden yelled and let off another shot but all it found was the bank. Fine dirt sprayed into the air.

'If it was anyone's fault then maybe the blame lies with your father,' Cole shouted and thumbed bullets into the chamber of the Colt. 'He turned you bad. That first time, whenever that was, that he covered up for you, taught you that money and power could overcome any problem. It was then that this all started. From that moment on you were heading for this day.'

Sam Bowden screamed and shot several times in quick succession but all his bullets went wild. He had fired in fury and he crouched down so that the bank covered him while he reloaded.

Cole quickly realized that Bowden was temporarily out of ammunition. He ran to the side of the road and jumped down into a ditch. He figured the ditch would lead him up to Bowden since it skirted the road and ran upwards.

'What say we make us a little deal?' Bowden yelled, and Cole used the cover of his voice to move forward. The bottom of the ditch was moist and his feet sank with every step, making a squelching sound as he pulled them free.

'What's the matter, Masters?' Bowden yelled. 'You lost your tongue?'

Cole froze, fearing that any moment now Bowden would realize he had moved and come looking for him. Cautiously he took a few steps forward and then rounded a corner. He could see Bowden up ahead, leaning over the bank trying to spot where he had got to.

Cole stood perfectly still, taking aim on Sam Bowden. 'Drop it,' he said.

Bowden spun around in surprise. He fired, but his bullet went far wide of the mark and Cole fired back before he could aim and fire again. Bowden spun around again, shot in the shoulder; he very nearly lost his footing but somehow he managed to stay upright. He fired again. His bullet did nothing but Cole's was much more accurate.

Sam Bowden yelled in pain as a bullet tore into his chest. His legs buckled beneath him but somehow he found the strength to fire again, sending a bullet whizzing dangerously close to Cole. Gritting his teeth against the pain he tried to stop his arm aching as he fired yet again.

Cole stood there like a statue and shot once more. He shot Bowden in the head, killing him instantly, sending brains and skull into the afternoon air.

'Now it's over,' Cole said. He went and removed the star from Bowden's shirt. 'Now it's over.'

22

Cole stood looking down at the grave marker.

It's been a year now, he thought. A year since Em passed, took that bullet up in the mountains. He bent and rubbed mould from the cross that was threatening to obscure the inscription he himself had carved.

Emlyn Royston Tanner,
Born: unknown. Died: 1879
A good friend sorely missed.
Now resting with his maker.

Behind him there was a double plot, containing both Clem and Sam Bowden. And, like Em's, the grave was well tended, with fresh flowers in the silver vase that sat below the headstone.

No one in town knew who tended the Bowden plot but Cole knew and kept the knowledge a secret.

Folk wouldn't understand.

He turned and walked away from the graveyard and met his wife, who was waiting at the gates. Together they walked down the hill towards town, Cole carefully supporting the heavily pregnant schoolteacher.

Other titles in the
Linford Western Library:

THE TOMBSTONE VENDETTA

Ralph Hayes

When Billy Clanton and his friends are murdered in Tombstone by the town marshal and his deputies, the growing tension between the local authorities and the ranchers spirals out of control. The once sleepy frontier town is mired in hatred, with bad blood and scores to settle on both sides. Families are torn asunder as the violence rages on. Will there ever be peace in Tombstone? Or will peace only come when one side reigns victorious?

LAND OF THE LOST

Dean Edwards

Young drifter Hal Harper's welcome to the town of Senora is to look down the barrels of the law — little knowing that the outlaw Tate Talbot and his gang are the elected sheriff and deputies. Talbot, with a wanted poster on his head worth a fortune, decides to collect his own bounty by killing the innocent Harper and claiming the drifter is the outlaw known as Diamond Bob Casey. Harper escapes — but only into the Land of the Lost . . .

THE LEGEND OF TORNADO TESS

Terrell L. Bowers

Author Amy Cole wants more than to write a story — she wants to live one. Her chance comes when she's asked to help to clear a doctor of murder. Amy's investigation takes her to Little Babylon, a bandit stronghold in the wasteland of New Mexico. Meanwhile, Whitney Scott trails a band of killers to Little Babylon and meets Amy. However, working together, Whitney faces an unknown assassin — and Amy's priority, over solving the murder, is to stay alive!

CONFEDERATE PAYDIRT

Robert Anderson

Jim Murphy plays high stakes poker — until he hears about the gold; Billy wants to avoid his old comrade, ex-Union Sergeant, Joshua O'Donnel; Seraphim Angel McCall is just greedy — and nobody trusts anybody. The unlikely four band together, searching for lost Confederate bullion. However, when Zachariah Holmes and his murderous band of Comancheros confront them, in the wastes of the sun-blasted desert, bullets fly. The gold may be there, but will anybody live to retrieve it?